Seven NIGHTS OF SIN

New York Times & USA Today Bestselling Author

KENDALL RYAN

Seven Nights of Sin
Copyright © 2019 Kendall Ryan

Copy Editing by
Pam Berehulke

Content Editing by
Elaine York

Cover Design and Formatting by
Uplifting Designs

Photography by
Lindee Robinson

ABOUT THE BOOK

He's the powerful CEO. I'm the know-it-all intern.

Things went further than they should have, but I don't have any regrets. Well, maybe just one . . .

I went and did the one thing he told me not to—fall in love with him.

Dominic Aspen is complicated, demanding, and difficult, and I want every ounce of this deliciously broken man. A man who fought to keep his twin daughters and has a hidden tender side.

I have seven days to prove my trust and devotion. Turns out money is a powerful drug, but love is even more addictive.

Seven Nights of Sin is the stunningly sexy and heart-pounding conclusion to *The Two-Week Arrangement*.

CHAPTER ONE

Dominic

P resley is standing on the curb as I pull up to the gas station. I took the Porsche, not the SUV; she doesn't get to see that part of my life anymore. She lost that privilege about the same time she destroyed whatever trust we had built, shattered it like a crystal glass thrown against a concrete floor. It's messy, the ugly remnants still there, mocking me by reminding me of what happened and of what we had.

I still feel so deceived, so hurt and angry. But I'm here.

I'm still not entirely sure why I'm here, but I guess it's because she sounded so desperate on the phone, the sound of tears evident in her shaky voice. Not that she told me much on the call, only that she needed me to come get her. Curious and a little bit worried, I called Francine to come over, then grabbed a jacket and took off once she arrived to watch the girls.

I had a lot of questions, and even more spring to mind now that I see how Presley is dressed. She's wearing the same little black cocktail dress and heels she wore on our weekend at Roger's lake house.

Was she on a date?

My hands grip the steering wheel harder. It shouldn't matter; we're broken up now. I don't even want to be involved with her anymore, but none of that reasoning stops the twinge of jealousy I feel low in my stomach.

When I get closer, I see her makeup is smudged beneath her eyes. She's been crying, either before or after her frantic phone call to me, I'm not sure. And she's shaking like a leaf. What the hell is going on? How long has she been standing outside? More importantly, why is she standing out here all alone?

It may be summer in Seattle but the nights, like tonight, can be chilly. Her arms are bare, but still, she waited out here. For me.

When I park beside the curb, she scurries to the

passenger door and quickly gets into the car.

"Thank you so much," she says through chattering teeth, rubbing her exposed arms. "I didn't know who else to call. I know it's late. I'm really grateful."

I nod in acknowledgment. I should ask where to drop her off, but for some reason, I can't bring myself to take Presley to her apartment and leave it at that with no explanation. Telling myself it's because I want answers first, I turn toward her.

"So, what's going on?" I ask. I deserve at least some answers as to why I was her first phone call, don't I?

She stares ahead, not meeting my eyes, fidgeting with her purse strap. "W-well, my phone was dead, and the only number I could remember was yours, so . . ."

"That explains why you called me, but it doesn't explain why you needed my help. I want to know what happened."

Although I'd never abandon a woman stranded alone at night, I make no effort to soften my tone. My genetic makeup won't allow me to ever walk away from or hang up on a female in need, but I also don't have to forgive her betrayal just because she's in trouble.

Presley's gaze drops to her lap and her hands wring her purse strap so hard, I'm surprised it doesn't break. "I . . ." She pauses, hesitating.

I say nothing, just wait. We can sit here all night if that's what it takes. The only sound is the subtle purr of the Porsche's engine. It's a sound that used to calm me. But tonight I feel anything but. On edge, anxious, pissed off, sexually frustrated—hell, maybe even a combination of all of them.

Finally, she mutters, "I was doing a gig for Allure."

My gut twists so hard at her admission that I'm glad I waited to start driving, because I'm pretty damn sure I'd have wrapped this car around a tree with the physical reaction I have to this bombshell. Rage burns hot inside me, and it takes a minute to respond because my heart is hammering so hard, blood roars through my ears.

"You what? Allure? Like as an escort?"

She winces. "I needed the money! I thought I'd lost my job, because of, well, the whole Genesis thing." She twists to face me, her eyes pleading. "Dominic, I'm so sorry ab—"

"Stop. We're not doing this right now."

Her mouth snaps shut.

After a tense few moments, I grit out, "We can talk about it later."

Surprise flits over her face. "At work?"

"No. Tonight. I'm taking you to my place." I pull back out onto the street.

A different kind of surprise flashes across her features now, mixed with emotions I can't read.

Is she happy about that? Apprehensive? Just plain confused? I don't know. I can barely sort out the chaos inside my own head, let alone try to figure out what's going on in hers.

But I do know the last thing I want to do is take her back to a darkened apartment, not knowing what the catalyst was for her to be out here, all alone, after having just left God knows what type of situation that would warrant her calling me from an out-of-the-way gas station. This possessive feeling I have over her is entirely inappropriate, but in this moment? I give zero fucks.

I'm driving too fast. But I'm angry, and hurt, and beyond frustrated with her.

Why would she have put herself in an escort-type situation? Why do I even care where she was tonight? Those files and the jump drive she had her bag are all I should give a damn about. I *am* still pissed about that, beyond pissed, but this . . . stings, in a different way.

And deep within my anger is a tiny grain of relief that even though she was with another man, in whatever capacity, at least he wasn't a man she really cared for. Which just makes me even more furious—this time at myself.

• • •

Back at home, I take a deep breath, trying to slow my heart, and guide Presley toward the guest room. She watches me with wide eyes, pausing in the center of the plush carpeting with her heels dangling from one hand.

"Get comfortable," I say in a gruff voice, then head straight to the kitchen to pour myself a neat Scotch. On second thought, I make it a double. I'll need some serious alcohol if I have any hope in hell of falling asleep tonight with this swarm of contradictory emotions fighting in my gut.

And with Presley sleeping just a few yards

away, whispers a voice from deep in the less-evolved parts of my mind. Here with me, in my home, where we once shared so many happy memories.

I drink like I'm forcing down medicine. No, I'm not going to dwell on her. I'm not happy she's here. Go the fuck to sleep and deal with it in the morning, like I told her. Stick to the plan.

Francine steps into the kitchen and watches me. I didn't even bother to turn on a light, and in the dim glow cast by the moon, I can see her frown as she watches me. She must have a million questions about what's going on between Presley and me, but I have exactly zero answers. It's a very unusual predicament for me.

"Thanks for coming in. I'm sorry it's so late," I say, my throat hoarse from the liquor.

She makes a sympathetic noise and crosses the room to stand before me. For a moment, I think she's about to hug me, which surprises me because Francine and I have never had any kind of physical contact. Even though she's always treated me with a motherly warmth, it's always lacked any affection, which has been just fine by me. But rather than hug me, she reaches around me and grabs her purse from the counter.

"Good night, Dominic. Try to get some rest. You need it." She touches my forearm once, pats it softly, and then disappears around me toward the door.

"Drive safe," I mutter into the darkness.

Once the tumbler is empty, I head back down the hall. But something slows me as I walk past the guest room.

It occurs to me that I never checked to make sure Presley was okay. What's wrong with me? That client clearly scared her—she called me begging for help—and I didn't even bother asking about what happened.

I need to know if he hurt her, did something to upset her. *Touched her.* There will be hell to pay with Allure if that prick did something to her. Their screening process is supposed to be rigorous, specifically to keep sick fucks away from their escorts.

The idea of Presley entertaining another man is an unpleasant one. I shake my head. *Dammit*, I don't care who she did or didn't fuck, taking care of her is just the right thing to do. I'd do the same for anyone in the same situation. Wouldn't I?

I'll just check on her quickly, I tell myself, *and then head to bed*. Just to see if she needs any help.

She's a guest, and she's my employee, something bad obviously happened tonight . . . it's the least I can do.

I ease open the door as quietly as possible and peek in. She's facing away, her dark hair spilled luxuriously over the pillow. Her side rises and falls in a gentle, even rhythm. Fast asleep.

I should leave now. So, naturally, I find myself seated on the edge of the bed because I've made some pretty stellar decisions when it comes to this woman, obviously.

Her lovely face is peaceful. As far as I can tell in the dim moonlight, there are no bruises or any other marks, thank God. The covers have slipped, revealing her bare shoulder and the strap of her dress. It's obvious she would sleep in her clothes, without anything to change into, and because I didn't even offer her one of my T-shirts to wear. *Real smooth, Dom.*

I carefully pull the top blanket back over her, and she sighs.

What am I doing?

I have no idea. Maybe I never did.

• • •

I must have fallen asleep sitting up, just like I used to do next to the girls' cribs when they were babies and restless, because I quickly wake at the sound of the toilet flushing. I grunt and rub my eyes before glancing at the clock on the nightstand. *Three in the damn morning. Terrific.*

Presley pads barefoot out of the en-suite bathroom, spots me, and freezes. "Dom?"

I clear my throat. Coming in here was obviously a mistake. I don't act like this . . . ever—but here I fucking am.

"I came to ask if you needed anything, but you were asleep."

She nods, not moving any closer.

"I guess I fell asleep too," I admit. "Are you okay?"

She moves to sit on the bed, giving me a wide berth. Because she doesn't want to be near me, or because she thinks I don't want to be near her? I do . . . which is precisely why I shouldn't.

"I'm okay," she says.

"What happened tonight?"

She looks down at her hands, stalling for time. "I went out with a client. I told you that. I needed the money." Her voice is small, barely above a whisper, the embarrassment about her financial situation obvious in her tone.

"And your client?" I ask, my voice cold.

She looks up, meeting my eyes. "He was an asshole."

Rage stirs in my veins. Knowing that she went out with another man shouldn't bother me this much, but it does. I was the first man to touch her, the first inside her. The intimate moments we shared meant something. Although apparently all that's behind her now.

"I see. So you've sucked two dicks now?" I ask.

Her face tightens, on the verge of crumpling. "It didn't get that far," she says, her voice choked and wavering. She swallows hard. "In fact . . . when he tried to push me into touching him, that's when I ran away."

I shouldn't have said that. It was mean and pointless, and it just leaped out of my mouth like a toad.

Feeling like an asshole, I look away. "Did he hurt you?"

She shakes her head. "He was really gross, but not violent."

"Did he touch you?"

"Yes. Not, uh, anywhere under my clothes, though."

I consider asking for his name, then decide it's better for me not to know or else I might hunt him down and kill him.

"Gia told me it would just be dinner," she says. "Just companionship."

"Then that's what she believed it would be. This piece of shit must have been trying to game the system by lying on his request form. Report him and enjoy the fireworks."

Presley manages a feeble *heh*. Her weak smile tugs at my insides. I can't spend all night in here or I'll do something I'll regret.

I stand up and start for the door. "Get some sleep."

"Dom?"

Her tiny voice stops me in the doorway.

"I really wasn't going to go along with Austin's plan. I'd never sabotage anyone's company like that, let alone yours. When he first approached me, I thought it was a happy coincidence. I thought he wanted to be . . . friends."

She wets her lips. "But then after a few get-togethers, he told me what he really wanted, and of course, it was all a setup from the very beginning. He was saying all these things about what happened with Aspen and Genesis that didn't match the official story. I just didn't know what to think about it all, so I took his dossier home to read later."

Instead of turning and walking away like I should, I ask coldly, "And the jump drive?"

"I was going to analyze the files on it and then hand it over to IT." Her eyes beg me to believe her.

"I want to believe you." I drag my hand over the stubble on my cheek with a loud, aggravated sigh. I'm just so drained. "Maybe I do. But I still don't know where we stand, whether I can trust you anymore." *Even if I wanted to.*

She presses her lips together, blinking fast, then nods. "That's fair. I just . . . wanted to tell you."

"I have to check on the girls, and you need to get some rest." At the threshold, I add a quiet

"Good night."

Everything should have already ended between us. But closing the door still feels like I'm tearing something fragile apart for good.

It scares me how much I hate it.

CHAPTER TWO

Presley

I'm frozen, staring at the guest room door. I can't move an inch, not even to bury myself under the covers in the bed behind me. To think, not long ago I was in *his* bed, thrumming with the amazing clarity of knowing I was exactly where I wanted to be, giving him a gift I'd held on to for someone special.

Oh God.

The knot in my gut tightens with each passing second. My mind is racing with questions, and not for the first time, I berate myself for being so damn stupid.

What was I thinking? How could I have been so blind?

I should have never taken that file from Austin.

He had seemed so harmless at first. He was nice to me, interested in my work, good with Bianca . . . but a complete parasite the entire time we spent together. The sheer arrogance of the guy—*no. Dammit.* My own arrogance. Why would I take the file if I knew that it would jeopardize my already unstable standing at Aspen Hotels? Why would I risk Michael's future like that?

Why hurt Dom?

That's the bigger question. Just when he was starting to open up to me, to trust me. He'd let me in—however briefly—and let me meet his daughters. I knew how big of a deal that was. He keeps them highly guarded from the public, the media, everyone. I was one of the few people he trusted to meet them.

And now I've made a real freaking mess of things.

I'm not one to let things lie, though. Especially not if I'm the one who dropped the ball. If there's a problem, I'm going to face it head-on. Still, I don't think I've ever been this unsure, this terrified about addressing a problem. This isn't quite a spat between coworkers, or even friends. I don't even know what we are, so there's no sure-fire way to approach this situation. Regardless, I know what I have to do. I need to try, at the very least.

I place a firm hand on the doorknob.

I can see through the crack of his bedroom door that Dominic still hasn't gone back to his room. *Good.* As I sneak down the hall, my feet pad lightly across the wooden floor. I can hear his murmuring voice, calming a scared little girl.

My heart falls from my throat to my belly. I wonder if the noise of our argument, discussion, whatever the hell it was, woke one of his daughters from a deep sleep. *Am I to blame?* I make a small promise to myself to make it up to her later.

I'm also struck at how, in the midst of his personal turmoil, Dominic still has to take the time to be a dad, to offer soothing words, to place his child's needs ahead of his own. My heart breaks a little more at the thought that I've hurt this man.

When I reach Dominic's room, I don't think. Instead, I pull my dress off over my head. And since I already removed my bra before getting into bed earlier, I'm in my birthday suit in less than a second.

Showing Dominic how sorry I am—showing him that I'm willing to put all my insecurities, my doubts, my freaking self-preservation aside to get him to trust me again—is the only thing on my mind. I'm offering myself up on a silver platter. Offering to fix this without words.

Sex is a language that Dominic knows well, and one I need to use to communicate what he means to me. Just like I felt backed into a corner to go to work for Allure to save Michael, this is my last shot to salvage my relationship with Dominic. My only chance.

God, I hope it works.

I slip under the silky sheets and fluffy duvet, and wait, one elbow propping myself up so I can watch the doorway. My heart hammers wildly behind my ribs.

His footsteps sound from down the hall, and my heart rate picks up.

This is it.

The look on Dominic's face when he enters the room is almost comical. He's so confused, his beautiful eyebrows drawn together, his stormy eyes fixed on mine. It isn't fair how this man can wear any expression and still look like some flawless male model on a billboard.

"Hey," he says, almost as a question.

"Hi."

Here goes nothing.

Before he can say anything else, I sit up, letting the sheet slip from my breasts. His gaze drops to my naked chest, his eyes widening slightly as my nipples tighten in the cool air. His lips part.

Bingo.

"Can you forgive me?" My voice is soft, barely above a whisper, and my self-confidence is gone.

"Presley . . ." His tone is so broken, I feel it like a sharp stab inside my chest.

"I promise. I promise I was never going to sabotage you. You have to believe that. If that's all that I wanted, I wouldn't still be here now."

I can't read his expression. God, I wish more than anything that I could just get one tiny peek into the mind of this exquisite, confusing man.

Not that he'd ever let me.

Dominic looks at me with dark, seeking eyes. He licks his lips, his thumb pressing against the lower one as he watches me. "What's your plan?"

"My plan?" Confused, I tilt my head.

His thumb slips away from his lip, and he nods. "What are you going to do to make up for it?"

Oh . . . my plan.

I rise to my knees, the sheet completely abandoning my bare flesh. I don't know where this confidence has come from, but I'm plenty aware of what my body does to his—and vice versa. Maybe this is what I need to do. Be brave and make him forget all the ugly, messy things that have happened between us.

I cock my head at him and smile, holding one hand outstretched.

Come here.

He remains stock-still, watching me, and *God, he's so beautiful*. So masculine and commanding, while I feel small and frightened and unsure. The balance of power is tipped entirely in his favor, and right now I don't care at all. He has all the control. Everything that happens next is up to him.

God, please let him choose me.

Dominic takes two steps forward, and then he practically attacks me, his mouth on mine in a hard, brutal kiss of passion. No matter how angry he may be, no matter how confused he is, right now I can tell that he wants me, that he wants to put all this behind us. And with the way his tongue sucks shamelessly on mine, he can have whatever he wants. I melt into his touch, my heart now hammering for an entirely different reason than it was a moment ago.

I clutch his dress shirt in my fingers as his hands sink into my hair, holding me close.

"You know—what they say," I whisper between gasping, open-mouthed kisses.

"Hmm?"

The fingers of his right hand slide up my thigh. I know what his destination is, and I can't wait to feel those fingers caressing me once again . . . readying me for his thick length.

"The bigger the—breakup, the better—the sex." I whimper, his kisses now almost bites against my throat.

This is going to work, Presley. This is actually going to work.

But then he pulls away.

"Dominic?"

The man before me wears an unreadable mask.

He steps back, releasing me. I can still feel the warm imprints of his hands, now suddenly exposed to the cool air of the room.

His breathing is ragged, his chest rising and falling quickly, and there's an unmistakable bulge beneath his zipper.

"I want you, Presley. You know that."

My throat tightens.

"But I can't trust you. And trust . . ." He swallows, his eyes locking onto mine. "It's everything to me."

"Dom—"

"Just stop. I've been burned before." His eyes are dark and unreadable, and I know that the moment has passed.

"Their mother?"

"Yes," he says, his voice hoarse.

I hate to press him on this, but my curiosity has always gotten the better of me. He's vulnerable. Now may be the only chance I'll get to peek inside.

I sit back on the bed and pull the sheet up to cover myself, while he remains standing beside the bed. "Who was she?"

He weighs my question for a moment, and I'm not sure if he'll answer. It wouldn't surprise me if he didn't. He's not exactly known for being the type to offer up personal details. But then his lips part and he meets my eyes again.

"Her name was Sara. She was an escort I hired for an event. We clicked, and I started requesting just her. It went on that way for a couple of months. Then we got careless, and . . ."

I clear my throat. "She got pregnant."

He nods. "She didn't want them. She didn't want to be a mother. She wanted her life back. But the paternity test said they were mine, so I paid her."

"Paid her?" I cock my head to the side. Dear God, the things this man does with his money . . .

"To give birth, rather than have the abortion that she wanted to."

Oh.

My skin feels cold and my heart hollow. I can see how much this hurts him to tell me. I can see it in his eyes and hear it in the tremor of his deep, full voice—now strained with emotion. I never wanted him to relive that devastation, but I'm the one who pushed him to the edge.

"I'm so sorry, D—"

"I think you should go."

There. I've really done it now. I've jeopardized my job, my brother's future, my . . . whatever this catastrophe of a relationship is.

I have no place here. Dominic's life is a complicated mess, and I've only scattered the pieces even more, like a selfish child.

It's time to grow the hell up, Presley. I screwed up, and now I have no choice but to live with the consequences.

Without a word, I stand. I put on my dress and panties under his watchful gaze, my fingers trembling, and head to the guest room where my bra lays on the floor.

After I gather my purse and shoes, I slowly make my way down the hall, past the girls' bedroom, and through the front door. The door clicks shut behind me.

Never once in my walk of shame—shame over everything I've done—does he try to stop me.

Why would he?

CHAPTER THREE

Dominic

After my roller coaster of a weekend, coming into work on Monday morning is a relief. The atmosphere at Aspen is fast paced and high pressure, as always, but it's also familiar. I'm in my element here. In control. Unlike in certain other areas of my life.

I grab a cup of coffee and settle in at my desk with an in-box full of emails, and release a heavy sigh.

My improved spirits last for all of an hour before Oliver pokes his head into my office.

"Hey, boss man," he says.

Looking up from my computer screen, I give him a wry look. "I've told you not to call me that." Even if I am his boss, he's also my best friend.

Oliver just shrugs as he strolls inside and settles into the armchair in front of my desk. "What's going on with Presley?"

My stomach tightens, but I train my features to remain calm. Oliver couldn't possibly know the extent of what's gone on between us.

Presley wouldn't have spilled the beans . . . would she? I wouldn't expect that of her, but given everything that's happened in the past forty-eight hours, I clearly don't know her as well as I thought I did. I never thought in a million years she could be bribed by the competition, or that she'd join the ranks at Allure.

Careful to control my tone, I reply, "What do you mean?"

"She's not here, that's what. And nobody's heard from her." Oliver scratches his head. "I guess that means you haven't either. Weird. I figured if she'd said anything to anyone, it would be you."

"Me?"

His eyes narrow. "Yeah. Her direct supervisor."

I sit back in my chair. "Right."

His eyes widen as he watches me.

I have no idea why she's not here. Is she too upset to work? That doesn't seem right. Knowing what I do about her personality, I would have guessed she'd at least call in sick, not just disappear.

Then I remember the comment she made when I rescued her two nights ago. She thought she'd lost her job. That I'd fired her. At the time, I'd been too focused on all the other crazy shit going on to address it.

"I'll give her a call right now and check on her," I say.

Oliver nods and crosses one ankle over his knee, apparently settling in for the long haul.

"I meant in private," I add.

He rises and walks out with a grunt. I'll deal with his moody ass later. Right now, all I care about is dialing Presley's cell.

After a few rings, she answers with a confused, "Hello?"

"You're not fired," I say.

"But I . . ."

"Get to your desk."

A long pause. "But . . ." Her tone wavers, and then firms. "Yes, sir. I'm sorry for the misunderstanding. I'll be right there."

She's as efficient as ever. In under half an hour, I hear heels tapping on the floor outside my office and a knock at the door. I call out a brusque "Come in."

Presley looks polished and beautiful in her black pencil skirt and white silk blouse. Of course she does—she's always lovely, no matter what she wears, and my body hasn't forgotten last night's interrupted make-out session and subsequent case of blue balls.

But I can't notice details like that anymore. I have to lock away everything we've done, everything personal we've seen about each other, and go back to just being her boss. Strictly professional. It's the only way.

Violating my trust isn't something that I can overlook, no matter the person, but I don't want to raise any suspicions at work, so it's better if she's here. Business as usual.

"Do you have a question?" I ask.

"Yeah, actually. I was surprised to get your call. I thought we were . . ." She looks around to make sure no one is in earshot. "You know, done."

"We are done—outside the office. But your internship isn't over yet."

She blinks. "I thought you said you didn't trust me anymore."

"I don't. However, the fact remains that your work here has been top notch, so I'd like to give you a chance to prove me wrong."

Plus, her finishing her internship here will mean fewer questions from Oliver and the rest of my staff, but I don't share that tidbit. It's been obvious to everyone that Presley is one of the most talented interns here, so firing her wouldn't make any sense.

A flurry of emotions flit through her eyes, then she suppresses a smile. "Challenge accepted."

I resist the urge to watch her walk away and instead force my gaze to return to my laptop. I seriously need to pull my shit together. What kind of boss is the last person to notice when their own intern doesn't show up?

Fucking hell. Oliver must know something's up, but I'll deal with that later.

Not ten minutes later, the intercom on my desk

beeps, and I almost groan. *For God's sake, what now?*

I press the button. "Yes, Beth?"

"There's a phone call for you from Mr. Harwood. Shall I put him through?"

I sigh and rub my temples. "Go ahead. Thank you."

Another beep, and Roger's jovial voice booms, "Morning, Dominic. Hope you're having a good day so far."

Not remotely. "Same to you," I reply with as much friendly cheerfulness as I can fake. "What's on your mind?"

"Well, I've been chewing over everything we've talked about, and I've gotta say, you make a damn compelling argument. I think I'd like to invest in Aspen's international growth."

This is everything I could have wanted. All those long evenings of elbow-rubbing have finally paid off. So, why aren't I doing a touchdown dance at my desk? Maybe I'm just too distracted by this whole Presley mess.

"That's fantastic news. Great to hear we've impressed you. I'll have Beth send ov—"

"Not so fast, son." Roger chuckles. "I want to at least see the property you plan to build on first. You know what they say about location."

"That's fair."

Looks like I can't put off that scouting trip any longer. But the idea of being so far away from Emilia and Lacey for so long is unpleasant enough that I've been pushing it back for months.

"There are a few spots in London I've had my eye on. How does your schedule look for, say, next week for a little trip across the pond?"

He laughs. "You get right to the point, don't you? Sure, I can make time. Surprise the missus with a little vacation."

"Then I'll see you there for high tea."

"Sounds terrific. I'll bring the paperwork. Speaking of significant others, will your lady friend be joining us? I certainly enjoyed talking to her a hell of a lot more than you." He almost belly laughs at his own humor while I inwardly groan.

Fuck. Presley is the main reason why Roger warmed up to the idea of working with Aspen Hotels. But I can't see her outside the office now, let alone jet off across the Atlantic for a week of pretend canoodling.

On the other hand, I'm so close to locking down this deal, I can taste it. I have to bring my A game, or in this instance, my P game . . . *Presley*. I refuse to risk blowing a massive deal it at the last minute over such a tiny detail.

"You still there?" he asks.

I clear my throat. "Sorry, I was just thinking. I'm not sure. I'll have to talk it over with Presley first." And make a brutally tough decision. Being in a hotel with her all week is bound to invite complications and send her the wrong message.

"Of course. And while I'd love to see her—" Roger's voice turns teasing. "I understand that a man needs to fly solo every once in a while."

Something about his choice of words rattles me. I've been flying solo for most of my life. I go out of my way to avoid messy entanglements, and look where that's gotten me.

I inhale and try to focus. "I'll email you as soon as I know. Have a good one." I hang up and lean back in my chair, my fingers steepled over my mouth in thought.

Roger just gave me the out I was looking for. I

can claim that I want to use this business trip as a girlfriend-free getaway. But now that I've thought about it . . . maybe bringing Presley to London with me wouldn't be such a bad idea. Maybe I can kill two birds with one stone.

Or maybe being alone with her will kill me. Who the hell knows at this point?

CHAPTER FOUR

Presley

"Wait, let me get this straight. Austin was like a spy?"

Bianca sits across from me in a small café a block away from our apartment. Her hands are tightly wrapped around her tea mug, her fingernails a deep navy blue. She leans forward like an angsty preteen, hungry to eat up some hot gossip.

"That's really not the important part," I say with a sigh.

I had my reservations about telling her any of this . . . but who else is there? It's not like I can tell Michael. He would blame himself for any pain he's caused me. He'd also freak out if he knew about my finances, but he needs to focus on school. Plus, he would think it's somehow his fault that my life is such a colossal shit show.

No. There's no way I can share any of this with him. It would break him.

I breathe in the steam of my herbal tea, willing it to calm my buzzing nerves.

"Hello? Are you still there?" Bianca's gazing at me with a confused expression.

I blink. I'd completely zoned out, spiraling down into the pit of my despair. Bianca reaches over and places a hand on mine. She squeezes it tightly, as if to squeeze the thoughts right out of me.

"Sorry, B, what did you say?"

"I asked if you were okay."

I laugh, feeling anything but okay. "Honestly? No." I let out a long, slow exhale. "I'm freaking out."

"Because of the job, or because of your hot boss who hates you?" she asks before taking a sip of her tea.

"Both?" I say, my voice tight with the tears I refuse to cry.

Bianca rubs her thumb across the back of my hand in a sweet gesture of comfort. I look into her eyes, searching for any bit of wisdom she may have to offer. I'll take just about anything right now.

"No situation is completely unsalvageable. Take me back to the beginning."

And so I do. I tell Bianca about meeting Dominic in the bar on that fateful night. About how my heart practically leaped out of my throat when he proposed the arrangement. A two-week arrangement of being his fake girlfriend. I don't tell her how well-versed he is in this kind of thing, preferring to only date high-end escorts. Even if he's no longer mine, I do still have some sense of wanting to protect him.

Not that Bianca would run to the media with that information. I know I can trust her—we've been besties since we were freshman roommates in college. But still, if that got out, it could crush him, and he'd know I was somehow involved with it getting out and that would damage our relationship beyond repair. It's already hanging on by a thread.

I explain how nervous and insecure I was before I realized that I'm a natural actress around men with heavy wallets, men who are capable of cinching a million-dollar deal over appetizers. And then, how electric every touch and caress felt when Dominic and I became physical. And finally, the moment I realized that he was a single father of two tiny children, and a truly fantastic one at that.

At this point, Bianca interrupts me. "Wait! He's a dad? He's like twenty-five!"

"He's twenty-six, actually."

"Well, I am no less amazed right now. A single dad to twins and running a huge corporation? That's impressive, to say the least."

Believe me, I know.

And the craziest thing is, he makes it look so effortless. Sure, he has Francine, but still. My runaway thoughts are interrupted by another question from Bianca.

"Where's the mama?" she asks, leaning forward on her elbows.

"Her name is Sara. She was . . ." I swallow. "An escort."

"*Excusemewhat?*" she blurts out.

"She was a—"

"No, I heard you. He knocked up an escort?" Bianca leans back in her chair as if to let this new information breathe in the space between us. "Wow."

"He has custody of the children."

"Why, because she was too coked up to care about her kids?"

"Bianca, it wasn't like that."

I'm surprised by how stern my tone is, but I mean it. I don't want Bianca to think any less of Dominic for the situation he was in. Or even Sara, for that matter. The whole situation is so fucked up, but who am I to judge?

"He really tried to take care of her. He wanted to do the right thing."

"Okay, okay. I'm sorry. I'm in hyper-defensive mode because my friend is hurting. This is all just so crazy. And honestly, who else do I direct all this anger toward? Tell me."

"I don't know." I moan, burying my face in my hands. "Me?"

"Presley, you did nothing wrong. Dominic is the dickhead here."

"Don't say that," I say, my voice muffled by my palms.

"Why? Give me one good reason."

"Because I think I have feelings for him." I

press my hands over my face, groaning.

There's a solid ten seconds of silence. I peek through my fingers to see Bianca studying me while she absentmindedly picks off her nail polish. She's waiting for me to say more, to divulge all my innermost thoughts.

Do I have to? I feel like all I do lately is ruin things. I used to think I had my shit together. Armed with my fancy new degree, I was on the fast track. I was going to storm the business world, take care of my brother, be everything to everyone . . . and now the only fast track that I'm on is to become the world's hottest mess of a failure. And it's only taken me a matter of weeks to get here. *Good times.*

"I just thought I had him pegged from the beginning, you know? I thought he was arrogant, unfeeling. Hot, but totally insufferable. And then he completely surprised me. He has this side of him that's so incredibly gentle and considerate. And when I got a glimpse of that—hell, when I got a piece of it myself—it . . . it was so good."

"The sex?" Bianca smirks, watching me.

"Obviously." Even though we only did it once. "But it was more than that," I say, shaking my head. "He was broken, and I got to see the parts of him that were still whole. You should have seen him cutting up grapes for his daughters."

"Well, I gotta say that that's not my definition of sexy, but hey, you do you."

We both fall into a flurry of giggles. I'm so relieved to have talked to someone about all of this. I've had it clutched tightly to my chest for so long, thinking that no one would understand. But Bianca would never judge me for feeling what I do.

"What do you think I should do?" I ask, clasping my hands under the table like I've got my heart in my lap.

Bianca chews her lip thoughtfully. "Well, he didn't fire you."

"True." The opposite, in fact. He demanded I get to my desk on Monday once he noticed I was missing.

"That's a good sign."

"Is it?" I'm not convinced. The way Dominic has been treating me feels like I'm only one minor misstep away from being blacklisted from the entire industry forever.

He wouldn't do that to you, would he? Not knowing makes the back of my neck feel hot and cold all at once.

"You're going to keep seeing him at work. Since he hasn't completely removed you from his life, you've got this opportunity before you. Maybe you can win him over again and he'll let you back in?"

After all of this?

Bianca sees the question in my eyes and puts up a hand as if to say, *stop right there.* "It's his loss if he's too stubborn to let you back in. Don't sell yourself short for a man, sweetie."

Let me back in . . . Those are apt words for what I'm looking for from Dominic now.

When I met him, he was a locked vault, and not just anyone was given the key. I was lucky enough to get a chance to connect with him on a level I never imagined possible.

Now I just want him to open the door again. Maybe then we can revisit what we had. The banter, the chemistry, the tenderness . . . before he ripped it apart and threw it in the trash.

"You've got this, Presley," Bianca says with a confident smile. "You're the strongest person I know. If anyone can figure out how to wade through this mess, it's you."

My lips turn up and my heart warms. If Bianca believes in me, then maybe I do have a fighting chance.

CHAPTER FIVE

Dominic

My flight to London and the hotel room are booked. Francine has confirmed she can stay in my apartment for a week. I'll pay double her normal fee as thanks for her trouble. She insisted I didn't have to, but she's going the extra mile at the last minute, and there's no one I trust more to care for my girls.

There's only one detail left to arrange. I almost buzz Beth, then think better of it and dial Presley's desk phone myself.

"This is Presley Harper, Operations Department. How can I help you?" she says.

"It's Dominic. Can you stop by my office for a moment?"

"Oh! Hi, Dominic. Um . . ." In the background

is some brief rustling and the sound of keys tapping. "Yes, I'll be right there."

I lean back in my chair and try to relax. It isn't long before I hear a knock. I don't get up, only call out, "Come in."

Today she's wearing a simple black sheath dress, but the hint of her curves beneath the supple fabric makes a painful knot form in my throat.

Presley shuts the door behind her as she enters, her brow creased quizzically. "You wanted to see me? Is something wrong?"

I don't blame her for being curious about what I want. It's not like we had a meeting scheduled, and for anything short of an emergency, I usually just email her, knowing she'll respond within an hour or two. But this matter deserves a face-to-face talk.

"No, nothing like that. I just had a proposal for you and thought I should extend it in person."

She blinks but says nothing, only watches me with those wide blue eyes and waits for me to explain.

"Would you like to sit down?" I ask.

Without a word, she lowers herself gracefully

into the leather chair in front of my desk.

Swallowing, I weigh my options for how to present this to her. I have to approach it with care if I want to avoid giving her the wrong impression. I keep my face and body language neutral, fully leveraging the cold, calculated persona that's served me well in so many business dealings. If she's searching for a hint of what I expect from her, she won't find it.

Steepling my fingers beneath my chin, I say, "Next week I'll be in London to scout potential building sites for Aspen's first international location and finally nail down an investment deal with Roger."

"We're expanding? And Roger's on board too?" She grins. "Wow, that's great news!"

"It is." Her delight is contagious, and I allow myself a small smile. Why not? We've won a big victory with an even bigger payout, after all. "But let me finish. I was thinking I should invite you to come along."

Excitement spreads over her face, her eyes widening and lips parting slightly. "Y-you want me to sit in on your meetings? Does this mean . . . we're okay?"

I fight to ignore how cute she looks with her face all lit up like that. I can't betray any hint of the affection that, despite my best efforts, still lingers in me. "Not exactly. You wouldn't be attending strictly as my intern. What I had in mind was more . . . selfish on my part."

Her smile vanishes.

Now it's my turn to search her and come up dry. I'm not too worried—I already knew this would be a gamble, and I doubt she'll go running to HR—but having no idea what's going on in her head grips me like nothing else.

At last, she says slowly, "What do you mean by that?"

"It's seven nights, Presley. You can do as you please while I'm busy during the day, but in front of Roger, out at dinner, we'll pretend we're still dating." I fix her with a sharp look. "Assuming you can handle that."

She sucks in a breath. Was that a tiny shiver or just my imagination?

"So . . . when you say 'pretend we're dating,' I assume . . ." Her voice is quiet. "I assume we won't be doing anything date-like for real."

"No. That time is over. If you accompanied me to London, it would be for work only. Plain and simple. You'll obviously be compensated handsomely for your time away."

Presley drops her gaze. She's trying to hide it, but I can tell she's hurt.

Hell, if it stings me to say those words, it must feel a hundred times worse to hear them. But I'd rather err on the side of being a little too harsh than lead her on. I can't make her think that this offer is about anything emotional, anything beyond keeping Roger in a happy, cooperative mood.

"Just to be crystal clear," I say, "I want to emphasize that you're absolutely free to say no. Your job doesn't depend on agreeing to this trip."

Sure, she came on to me a few days ago, but for all I know, maybe she's totally over the idea of sleeping in a hotel room with me ever again. The thought triggers a twinge of hurt that I immediately squelch. I can't unduly influence her decision just because she thinks it's what I want . . . even though I do want it. So damn badly.

She still doesn't respond, just keeps studying my office carpet, looking torn. I can practically hear the gears spinning in her agile brain.

After another few moments of silence, I wave my hand airily. "There's no rush. You have a few days to think it over. My flight doesn't leave until—"

"I'll do it." Her tone is firm.

I blink. "What?"

Presley looks up again, still unsure, but determined. "I want to go to London with you."

She's caught me off guard. I didn't plan on that. I expected hesitancy, and instead she's given me urgency. I hate it . . . and love it too.

"Are you sure? I wouldn't be angry or let it affect our work relationship if you'd rather not."

"I know," Presley replies, like it's so obvious it goes without saying. "You wouldn't hold my career hostage just to get your way. You're not the kind of man who'd do something like that. I trust you . . ." She hesitates. "And I want you to trust me again."

She said *want*. Not *need*. Maybe I'm reading way too much into one little word.

Or maybe I'm not.

"What else do you want, Presley?" I can't resist

asking.

I tell myself it's not because I'm desperate to hear about her feelings—I just need to know for sure why she's agreeing to do this again. Is it entirely about earning her way back into my good graces, or is there more to it?

Pink creeps over her cheeks, but her voice is strong when she answers. "I'm not sure."

I purse my lips, then slowly nod. That's fine. Lust isn't dangerous in and of itself. The most likely scenario is that nothing will happen between us. And worst case? Say we do fall into bed together. Two mature adults can fuck without things getting weird and complicated, right?

"Okay. I'll have Beth reserve an extra plane ticket for you."

"What about the hotel?" she asks.

The corner of my mouth twitches up. "We won't need two rooms. You'll be staying in mine, remember?"

"Oh. Right. Of course." Her blush deepens.

I suppress a smile. "You can go back to work now."

After she's gone, I'm still staring at the door, suddenly not sure whether I made a genius win-win decision or a huge mistake. There's a very fine line between the two when it comes to Presley.

Can we really prevent emotions from getting involved here? I have no freaking clue, but I guess I'm about to find out.

Sighing, I shake my head. I'm way overthinking this—everything will be fine. *It's just to please Roger*, I tell myself.

At the very least, her company let me unwind from the hectic work that awaits and keep my mind off all the miles between me and home. Being away from my girls displeases me, and so any distraction will be a welcome one.

And I can't think of a better distraction than Presley in my bed.

CHAPTER SIX
Presley

"London is colder than Seattle, right?" I ask Bianca. She's lounging across her bed next to an impressive pile of sweaters in all shapes and colors. I leave for England with Dominic this afternoon, and in my distracted state, I've procrastinated packing the necessities. Like clothes. And toiletries. Which means I've emptied my suitcase and duffel bag onto her bed so she can help me pack.

Bianca pulls out her phone and scrolls briefly. "The weather app says it will be rainy. That doesn't necessarily mean cold, though. Sixties during the day and fifties at night."

"Hmm, all right. So maybe something a little breathable. Like this?" I hold up my favorite, a peach-colored cardigan in a clunky knit.

Bianca squints at it. "I don't think that's gonna be breathable enough."

"Really? I like it," I say, examining the texture between thumb and finger. I wore this cardigan through most of my time at Brown. It's been through some of the best and worst times of my life, from late-night essay-writing to early mornings at my favorite coffee shop.

"Presley," Bianca says, sitting up with a huff. "You don't need sweaters. You need lingerie."

"What?" I practically snort.

"Didn't he say you *wouldn't* be there strictly for business? I'm just reading between the lines." She wiggles her eyebrows in my direction.

"Just because I won't be there only for business doesn't mean I should only pack underwear."

"It's not underwear . . . it's *lingerie*. I know you have some. I've seen it."

She's right. She was there when I bought it. We'd gone to a discount boutique to look for something for her latest sexcapade. Naturally, I ended up in a dressing room as well. I remember turning around, looking at myself in the mirror, admiring the way the lacy pink bodysuit hugged my slight curves. Although it took me a minute to get used to it, I liked how it looked on me. The sheer silk fabric caressed my skin like a kiss. My nipples were almost completely visible, perky and curious in this new getup. The thong sat high on my hips, with garters stretching down my thighs. Looking over my shoulder at my reflection, I knew I had to buy it—even if I had no one to wear it for.

"I've never worn those," I admit.

"Never? We got them months ago, Pres. It's now or never," she says, peeking inside my duffel bag. "Where did you stash 'em?"

I slide past her and pull out a gift bag from where I stored it. I open it, and we both peek inside.

"Tags still attached. Wow, you really never wore these."

I shrug. "Never had the inspiration to."

"What about now?"

I chew on my lip. I can very clearly imagine the look on Dominic's face if he were to undress me and find this underneath. The way his eyes would grow dark and his lips would part . . . *God*, my heart rate kicks up just thinking about it.

"I guess I am a little more inspired now," I admit.

"Hell yeah, you are. This is an incredible deal. You get to literally just laze around in one of the most beautiful cities in the world, all expenses paid, with a gorgeous man."

I snort and shake my head. I'm joining Dominic on this business trip as a sign of good faith. I want to prove to him that I'm worthy of a second chance, and if he wants me to come along, of course I'll go.

I have nothing holding me back here. And if this internship leads to a full-time position, the perks will be absolutely unbelievable. Maybe I'll fall in love with London, and even take Michael on a trip there someday. We could get tickets to the Royal Ballet, and spend the evening exploring the cobblestone streets . . . *wow.* My belly swirls with butterflies. This trip may be the worst decision I've ever made, or it may very well be the best. Only time will tell.

Bianca plants a kiss on my cheek. "Lucky duck. Just give me a shout when you're ready to go."

"You don't have to drive me. I can just get an Uber."

"Hey. I'm your friend. I want to at least see this guy before I let him take you across the Atlantic." With a wink, Bianca leaves me alone to finish packing.

My passport gets stuffed into my purse along with a pack of gum and a mystery novel for the plane ride. And into my suitcase goes plenty of sweaters to keep me warm, plus the lingerie in case things get hot.

• • •

Later, I roll my suitcase down to Bianca's little sedan, and we make the short drive to Dominic's luxury high-rise building.

"Okay, I have to ask. Are you sure you want to go through with this?" Bianca's hands are on the wheel and her foot is on the brake pedal. We've just arrived outside of Dominic's apartment building and I'm about to step out.

My hand slips from the lock on the door. "What do you mean?" I'm not used to Bianca being the voice of caution in our friendship. Actually, she's the opposite.

She lowers her sunglasses to the tip of her nose. "I know things have been shaky . . . between work and Mr. Man. I just want you to be sure about it. You don't have to go if you don't want to."

I sink back into my seat, grateful for her concern. "I'll admit, I'm kind of nervous. This isn't really me . . . or it isn't who I thought I was." I meet her eyes, continuing in a braver voice. "But now, I'm learning things about myself on the daily. This new Presley is someone I'd like to get to know a little better. So I figure, why not follow my instincts and go on an all-expenses-paid trip with the hottest guy I've ever met?"

Bianca throws her head back and laughs at that.

"And," I say, "I feel like leaning into this."

"The adventure?"

"Yeah." And the guy.

Bianca leans over and wraps me in her arms, and for a second, I feel safe and warm and loved. After the tumultuous few days I've had, it's nice. Having her approval during this wild chapter in my life is everything to me. I squeeze her tight.

"I'm thankful for you," I say, finally pulling back.

"Aw, I'm thankful for you too. Now go get some dick."

I bark out a laugh and exit the car. *Yeah, right*

. . .

Unfortunately, Bianca doesn't get to examine Dominic in person like she wanted. After being let in by the doorman, I ride up to the twelfth floor alone, just me and my worn-out suitcase. I pause at his front door, my fist hovering inches from the door.

Come on, Presley. It's hardly leaning in if you can't even knock on his door.

Before I can make a decision, the door suddenly opens.

"Thought you'd be there," Dominic says, those sharp eyes appraising me. "Come in."

I follow him inside, taking note of the comfortable clothing he's wearing for our flight. I don't think I've ever seen him in a pair of jeans. But, *damn*, his tight glutes are just as awe-inspiring in denim as they are in dress pants. And to make everything worse, the cotton T-shirt he has on perfectly hugs his broad shoulders and firm biceps.

I can't help but wonder what he'd look like peeling it off.

I don't have a lot of time to ogle this new look before I'm distracted by Lacey and Emilia's small voices down the hall. They're not the cheerful voices I remember from my brief visit with them.

Of course, they wouldn't be happy to lose their father for an entire week, I get that. They must be so confused. Work trips aren't really within the realm of a two-year-old's understanding. I wonder how Dominic is feeling, having to leave his two little girls for an extended trip like this.

"Stay here," he says, relegating me to the front hall. He disappears around the corner, his voice a low hush compared to the whimpers of two toddlers.

Despite his order, I tiptoe after him, leaving my suitcase at the door. Curious to see what the interaction with his daughters will be, I peek around the corner.

"Don't go." Lacey whines, her tiny hands clasped around Dominic's fingers, who crouches before her.

Emilia sits sulking on the floor next to Lacey, her eyes wide and wet with tears. I can hear Francine bustling around in the kitchen, giving the family the space they need for this tearful moment.

"I'm going to miss you both too," Dom murmurs, kissing each little girl on top of the head. "You have to promise to call me every night, okay?"

The girls nod vigorously, their curls bouncing

around their faces. My heart warms at the sight. Dominic so easily made his girls feel better—not by being patronizing or cliché, but rather by admitting his own feelings to them.

If only he were like this with people his own age.

He turns to see me watching him, and my breath catches. "Let's go."

The limo ride to the airport is awkward and quiet. We sit in silence, a stark contrast to our more recent highlights in limos. He barely speaks to me at all, even when we arrive at the airport. We only make eye contact once, when he offers to lift my luggage onto the counter for me.

"Please," I say, my voice cracking with disuse.

His gaze seems to pass right through me, as if I'm merely a stranger in line he happened to do a favor for. Now, as we make our way down the aisle to our first-class sleeping pods, I'm itching to speak to him.

Have you been to London before?

Where will we be staying?

What's going on in your head right now?

There are so many unanswered questions desperate to slip out of my mouth and onto my growing list of regrets. But there's no opportunity for even casual conversation when he slides into the seat behind mine.

He doesn't want to talk to me; he's made that plain. And he's making it abundantly clear exactly what his expectations are concerning me.

Then why the hell am I here?

I turn away from his pod, refusing to waste any more time staring at his profile. If he wants to acknowledge me, he will. I won't beg for his attention.

No, I'll eat my dinner in silence and watch a mind-numbing movie about someone with bigger problems than my own, or I can read the book I brought with me and get lost in the pages. I won't spare another regretful thought about this situation I've willingly placed myself in.

As the plane takes off and rumbles with turbulence during the ascent, I sink into my seat and close my eyes, welcoming the escape of the roaring noise to drown out my own thoughts. Even as I slip off into sleep, I can't help but wonder . . .

What will tomorrow bring?

CHAPTER SEVEN

Dominic

We touch down at Heathrow around dawn and take a taxi to our hotel, a ritzy affair in the heart of downtown. Once we're checked in, I disappear into the bathroom without a word, leaving Presley to unpack and wander around the opulent suite.

With only an hour to get ready for a packed day of meetings, I have no choice but to be efficient here. I shave, shower, comb my hair, and dress in a fresh suit without paying much attention to her.

At least, I pretend not to, because I can never stop myself from noticing Presley, no matter how hard I try. I can feel her big blue eyes following me as I move about the suite.

I know I'm being kind of a dick, but the gaping hole where our trust used to be still gnaws at me, and I don't particularly feel like talking shit out. It's not something that can be solved with a few words anyway. Besides, I have the excuse of a tight schedule to use in my arsenal of avoidance techniques. So I continue saying as little as possible.

"Hey, Dom," Presley says quietly.

"What is it?" I don't look at her, busy tying my shoes.

"Never mind, you're in a hurry. Let me know when you're coming back, and I'll make sure to be here."

I give her an affirmative grunt. The last I see of Presley is her sitting on the edge of the bed, still watching me. Then the door closes, and I leave her behind, still wondering what she was going to ask me about.

My first stop is breakfast at the very posh Ramsay Terrace with a pair of top real estate agents who will pitch the living hell out of their property before taking me to view it. I order a full English breakfast with all the trimmings—I won't have time to grab much more than a bagel for lunch—and plenty of coffee. Correction, loads of coffee, because even a first-class pod can't negate the fact that a bumpy airplane ride is nowhere near as restful as sleeping in my own bed, near Emilia and Lacey.

That's not the only reason I didn't sleep well. I was too aware of Presley just down the aisle, of her beauty and our unresolved tensions. It's too bad I couldn't have breakfasted with her instead of chattering salespeople. If I weren't so damn busy this week, I could have shown her around my favorite spots in London . . .

No. I catch myself. Even if my time were my own, I still couldn't. That's not what this trip is about. I didn't bring her along for some fucking romantic getaway.

Still, I feel a little bad about ditching her to fend for herself. I should have at least fed her before leaving.

Oh, for God's sake. She's a grown woman. I made sure she knew to charge anything she needed to the room, ensuring she could take care of herself, and beyond that, she's more than smart enough to figure it out on her own.

"Don't you agree, Mr. Aspen?" one of the brokers asks.

I shake myself out of my thoughts. "My apologies. I guess I'm not completely awake yet. Can you repeat that?"

I manage to focus on business for the rest of the meeting and the tour afterward. Which is just as well, because the location is absolutely stunning with a view of the bustling city beyond the iron gates where a tower once stood.

In a taxi bound for my second appointment, I pull out my phone and dial Frank, the head of Aspen Hotels' legal department. It's a phone call I've been meaning to make for days. If nothing else, I can at least address the problem that started this whole shitstorm.

"It's Dominic," I say. "A man named Austin asked one of our employees to infect Aspen's computer systems with a virus. He was working for Genesis Software. I need you to get in touch with Genesis about this. Tell them to back off—preferably fire this Austin guy too, but I'll take what I can get—or else we'll press charges for attempted sabotage."

A pause. Which is impressive; it takes a lot to rattle Frank. "I'll take care of it right away, sir. In case this escalates, do we have evidence?"

"Yes. In the top left drawer of my desk, you'll find a flash drive containing the virus and a folder marked *Genesis*."

"And who was the employee he approached?"

I hesitate. Do I want to subject Presley to interrogation? She didn't actually do anything, at least based on what she divulged, and at this point, I think I believe her when she says she never intended to. Just because this whole incident has scared me straight, so to speak—reminding me how important it is not to let anyone get too involved in my personal life, it doesn't mean she deserves to get tangled up in legal repercussions.

Finally, I say, "I'd like to keep her out of this."

"I see," he says slowly, in a tone that means he doesn't.

"If we do end up taking Genesis to court, I'll talk to her about testifying, of course. But for now, call it an anonymous tip. I don't want to punish employees for reporting trouble."

"All right. Anything else you need?"

"That's all, thank you." I hang up.

A few minutes later my cell rings again, and I glance down as the taxi pulls to a stop. It's Frank. *That was fast.* Frowning, I climb out of the car and into a light drizzle of rain.

"Yes?" I head under the awning of a nearby

building, my phone pressed to my ear.

"Sir, I thought you'd want to be made aware—Austin Champlain isn't an employee whose employment would be easily terminated. He's the son of Genesis Software's owner."

"I see."

No wonder the kid had balls—he's got a huge stake in making sure Genesis doesn't fail.

I step inside the glass-and-chrome building, shaking the rain droplets from my briefcase. "That doesn't change things on our end, although I guess the suggestion that they fire him won't be met well."

"No, sir, I don't see how it would. But I'll make the call and keep you posted."

"I appreciate that, Frank. I'm in London all week, so make sure you call my cell, and leave a voice mail in case the time difference gets in our way."

"Absolutely. Enjoy your trip," he says before clicking off.

• • •

My day continues how it began—in a whirlwind of sales meetings and on-location visits, until twilight falls and it's too dark to keep looking at properties.

The last group of agents insist upon treating me to dinner at their favorite restaurant, Dalloway, which I happen to know is one of the most expensive places in London. It's obvious that they're trying to butter me up, but why not? It might be a chance to get a better deal out of them.

Unfortunately, Roger and his wife won't arrive in London until later tonight, which means I don't have an excuse to bring Presley, though part of me still wants to. But we head out right after leaving the last property—an undeveloped strip of land far outside of the city center.

"I hope we've made you feel welcome," says the jowly man seated next to me, whose name I can't remember for the life of me.

I force my most winning smile. "Except for the jet lag, everything has been amazing."

The others chuckle politely.

Damn, that joke wasn't as funny out loud as it was in my head. I'm off my game.

While I'm more or less satisfied with how the

day has gone, I'm still exhausted and very much in the mood for a pick-me-up. Something to relax me, something to help me work off this excess stress and my foul mood. And I know exactly want I want.

Struck by inspiration, I text Presley.

```
I'll be done in one hour. Meet me
at the hotel bar. Don't wear any
                          panties.
```

It's bold of me—and who knows, she might not comply with my demand. In fact, she'd have every right not to. But something tells me the game Presley and I have been playing isn't nearly done, and that she'll be tripping over herself to please me. At least, that's what I'm hoping.

Just the prospect of what I have to look forward to puts me back in shape for the rest of dinner. When the waitress comes by to pick up our plates and asks if we'd like anything else, Jowly Man nudges me.

"How about it?" he asks. "A few cocktails, Dalloway's famous desserts—all on our agency's tab, of course. My personal favorite is the blood orange cake with chocolate mousse."

"As delicious as that sounds . . ." I stand up with an apologetic dip of my head. "I should actually get going. I have an early morning tomorrow."

And a much more tempting dessert waiting for me at the hotel.

CHAPTER EIGHT

Presley

So far, my experience of London hasn't made it past the view from the hotel room window. Although you really can't call this a hotel room at all. First, it's much larger than Bianca's entire apartment.

There's a formal entryway with crystal vases containing fresh-cut flowers, gleaming marble floors, then a formal sitting area with teal-colored velvet chairs and elegant paintings on the wall. The living room boasts a gray sectional sofa and a large flat-screen TV. A bar area is beyond that, with a wall of windows that overlook the city, and then a private bedroom with a massive adjoining bathroom. The bed is positively oversize, and the slate-colored carpeting is the plushest I've ever felt. This place is a dream. Bored, I've already filled my cell phone's camera roll with pictures of its opulence.

I don't know why Dominic's wealth still surprises me; he is a billionaire, after all. But I guess I haven't wrapped my head around that just yet.

Sighing, I sit perched on a tufted stool in front of the floor-to-ceiling windows in the bedroom, gazing out at the bustling city below. I'm not complaining. It's a spectacular view. Our hotel stands tall, towering over the dense fog of the city. The skyline here is so different than that of Seattle. But even though the buildings are different sizes and shapes, the blue-gray hue of the city reminds me of home.

So far today, I've napped and eaten room service, twice, and surfed the channels on the TV—amused by the posh accents of the newscasters—and have been content, for the most part, to sit taking in the view. But it's been hours since Dominic took off to do his business in the city, and I'm getting increasingly antsy as the minutes tick by.

I'm not used to napping during the middle of the day, nor am I used to having so much downtime to myself. Even before college, I've always operated at 110 percent, balancing my studies with work and a social life.

I never knew it would be so hard to actually relax. My only excuse is that there is quite literally nothing for me to do here but laze around.

If I'm going to be confined to the hotel, I may as well make the most of it. The freestanding bathtub is massive with all sorts of bubble bath concoctions to choose from. I select the one called Peachy Clean, listening to the satisfying *glug-glug-glug* as I pour it into the steaming water. One foot at a time, I submerge myself in the bath.

Holy shit. This is heaven.

I let my back slide against the warm ceramic, an involuntary sigh escaping my lips. As a twenty-something always on the brink of breaking the bank, I *never* have the luxury of taking a bath. My morning routine is simple—get up, take as fast a shower as I can, and get out. My showers aren't even enjoyable, since I'm usually saving the hot water for Bianca, cognizant of my couch-surfing status. To make it worse, the pipes in her building are old and finicky. I'm lucky if there's decent water pressure.

I sink deeper into the bubbles, willing this moment to last forever. I can barely remember the last time I took a bubble bath . . . God, I must have been only five or six years old. Our mother always bathed Michael and me together, probably because we were so inseparable at that age.

Michael.

I should buy him a present while I'm here. He'll totally flip out when he learns I've been to London. What should I get him? More importantly, how will I explain this trip? I can't exactly tell him that I'm accompanying my megalomaniac boss on a business trip as his fake plus-one.

No, I'll just tell Michael what he wants to hear. It was a work trip. I was chosen to accompany my boss. (I'm his intern, after all.) We stayed in a fancy hotel with huge windows and complimentary room service—in *separate* rooms. I had a lovely time.

At least that last part is true so far.

Once I'm clean and shaved and my fingers look like pale little raisins, I wrap myself in a towel and re-enter the bedroom to get dressed. It's already past six o'clock. Is tonight the night to wear lingerie? Should I put it on now? Is it something women usually change into later in the evening? *So many questions about one tiny article of clothing.*

"Worry about it later," I grumble to myself.

I take the time to dry my hair but don't bother with any makeup. Then I slip on a pair of leggings and a loose T-shirt. There's exploring to be done first. I'm not supposed to leave the building, but surely there's some wiggle room in that restriction.

On the first level of the hotel, I find a tiny gift boutique that sells pleasant and affordable little trinkets, ranging from functional to simply ornamental. I find a magnet for the Royal Ballet. *Perfect.* It's just within my budget too.

Should I get anything for Bianca? What about for Dom's girls?

I'm certain that Dom would be extremely uncomfortable with that. I snort at the imaginary scene playing out in my mind—me, giving tiny snow globes of London to those wide-eyed, beaming angels while Dominic sweats from a distance.

My phone buzzes in the pocket of my leggings. I pull it out to find a message from the devil himself.

Meet me in the hotel bar in one hour. Don't wear panties.

Heat floods my cheeks and belly all at once. He *can't* be serious. But that's the thing about Dominic—he's always serious.

Oh my God.

I pay for the magnet with trembling hands, instantly forgetting my plans to shop for anyone else. I head straight for the elevator, ride it up to our floor, and fumble with the door key.

Once inside, I toss the magnet on the table and dump the contents of my suitcase on our shared bed. The little black dress I brought has miraculously survived the trip without any wrinkles. *Thank goodness*. I tug off the leggings and T-shirt and put them and the rest of the clothes I've scattered away.

Taking the dress over to the full-length mirror, I pull it over my body, smoothing the material over my breasts and hips. I'll have to run a brush through my hair and put a little color on my lips—

But first . . . I slide the dress up my thighs, slipping my hands underneath. My skin is silky soft, freshly shaved and moisturized from my bath. Imagining Dominic's hands on my skin later makes my entire body break out in goose bumps.

I hook my thumbs around the lacy underwear, pulling them down inch by inch until I can step out of them. Looking at myself in the mirror, I take in my long hair hanging over one shoulder, my breasts round and firm within the bodice of my dress, and the feeling of nothing between my legs . . .

Shit, I'm already turned on. From a text. Jesus.

I check the clock. I have forty more minutes to get ready. With how excited I am, I could probably get ready in ten.

Instead, I take my time in the bathroom, applying my eyeliner in a perfected black stroke, and add a little highlight here and there to my skin. The final touch is a swipe of pink lipstick. The gloss slides across my lips with purpose, painting my mouth a striking pigment a few shades darker than my natural coloring.

With my hair brushed and lips plump, I'm ready to handle whatever Dominic has planned. I can't help but rub my thighs together, noticing the lick of cool air that meets my bare flesh whenever my dress swishes.

One last glance in the mirror, and I'm ready— ready for whatever this evening throws my way. Although if Dominic has plans for us to entertain investors with me in this state, I'm fairly certain all my composure will vanish.

By the time I make it down to the hotel bar, my heart is hammering against my ribs, and I'm eager to see Dominic.

Composure, Presley.

My heels click on the dark tile of the bar floor. The lighting is dim and sultry, the result of low-hanging lanterns and tea-light candles strewn randomly across the small tables. I pause, uncertain if he's here yet.

"You're early. Good."

I practically jump out of my dress.

Dominic's lips are against my ear, and his hand is on my hip. I can feel the warmth of his body passing across the inches of empty space between us.

I swallow. Can he feel that I don't have underwear on? That I obeyed his commands?

"Being early is being on time," I say, impressed with how steady my voice is.

Who is this woman, with her straight back and unwavering charm? I don't know her, but I love her.

Without touching me again, Dominic leads me to the far corner of the bar counter. We sit as the bartender places a glass of dark liquor and a glass of bubbly before us. Dominic must have placed the order before I even arrived.

Okay, why is that hot? I sit down, acutely aware of how nervous I am. Dominic sits next to me, raising his glass to his full lips.

Which Dominic am I getting tonight? The confident CEO of a multimillion-dollar conglomerate? The soft-spoken, sensitive father with a broken heart? Or the insatiable sex god I've recently come to know and crave?

Based on his criteria for my wardrobe this evening, I'm guessing it's the latter.

"How was your day?" he asks, his lips twitching with a smile as he watches me. "Did you keep yourself entertained?"

Nodding, I reach for my glass of champagne and take a slow sip. I can feel his eyes on me the entire time, that kissable smirk still plastered across his mouth. "I made do."

"That's good to hear," he says, his tone low.

"And how about you? Did the amazing Mr. Aspen lock down any deals today?" I bat my eyelashes for effect, and he laughs. God, that laugh. I've missed it more than I thought possible.

This feels a little surreal right now—us flirting like this when he's barely spoken to me since I walked into his penthouse. Just days ago, all hope seemed lost. Maybe rules on heartbreak and betrayal don't apply when you're on a different continent. Who the hell knows. I feel so out of my element and consumed, but there's one thing I'm certain of—Dominic is staring at me.

As his dark blue eyes roam over me, examining every curve hidden by my dress, warmth spreads across my chest and neck. I return the favor, enjoying his look for the day—a slightly stubbled jawline, a navy-blue suit jacket, and a matching tie now pulled loose from his throat. He takes off his jacket, folds it, and sets it on the bar. I would be lying if I pretended I didn't want to kiss every inch of him—starting with his full mouth, and then down the thick column of his throat.

I don't have long to fantasize about touching him because he beats me to it.

I almost don't feel the brush of his fingers on my knee, his touch is so soft at first. But then more firmly, his hand presses against my leg, his thumb rubbing pulsing circles into my skin. I don't break his searing eye contact, afraid that I'll lose him to some passing thought or whim if I let go of him now. And there's no way in hell I want that hand pulling away.

He does move his hand, though, but not away from me. Instead, his fingers inch up beneath my dress, caressing my inner thigh.

I draw in a breath, realizing what he's doing, and squirm when he pauses just before discovering my lack of panties. While my heart hammers against my ribs, he casually takes a sip of his drink before setting it down, and then his hand inches higher.

I panic for a moment, glancing down at my lap. My dress covers everything still, even if I do feel exposed. With the cover of the bar, no one would know what he's doing. What *we're* doing. And I never expected it, but the secret thrill of being discovered makes my blood heat even more.

When I part my thighs a little, Dominic makes a low groan of approval and his fingers brush against my center.

"I see you've followed my instructions perfectly."

I gasp out a breath and give him a shaky nod. "Of course, Mr. Aspen."

He shakes his head in disapproval. "Dominic."

I lick my lips. "Right. Dominic." I recall how he corrected me my first few days at Aspen Hotels, telling me to call him Dominic instead of Mr.

Aspen. I was only trying to be cheeky just now—trying to regain some of the control in this crazy situation.

His fingers part me, his index and ring fingers sliding up and down my soft folds while his middle finger teases my center. He presses deeper, and I shudder and whimper audibly, finally breaking eye contact. I take a long swallow of my champagne, trying to focus on the sensation of the bubbles on my tongue rather than the sensation of his finger finding my clit.

Well, that's obviously impossible.

Dominic is skilled—perhaps too skilled—at foreplay. His touch is soft and gentle and wholly focused on my pleasure. He knows exactly what to do to bring me right to the brink.

My fingers clutch the cool granite of the bar to avoid rocking my hips against his hand. I'm remembering exactly how it felt to have him press inside me, and I want nothing more than to—

"Dom, is that you?"

My heart stops.

A man stands just behind us, his hand on Dominic's shoulder. Dominic turns and smiles broadly, but he doesn't remove his hand from its spot between my legs.

"Jerry? It's been so long."

Oh God, don't shake his hand, don't shake his hand, don't shake his hand.

He fucking shakes his hand.

Luckily, with the one *not* covered with my sticky sex nectar.

He hasn't removed his hand from between my legs, and I can't decide if I want him to or not. I just pray it's not obvious what we're doing.

Before I can even process what's happening, Dominic glides one confident finger inside me. I clear my throat to hide the squeal I make, then snatch Dominic's jacket and hold it tightly over my lap.

"You look great. And who is this?"

Fuck my life.

I turn to Jerry with a with a terrified smile. He has thin blond hair and the appearance of a man who could definitely get you fired with one wrong look. Rather than speak, I just smile, knowing I can't possibly open my mouth for fear of whimpering like a horny idiot.

"This is Presley. She's accompanying me on a business trip. What the hell are you doing in London? I thought you relocated to Amsterdam."

"Oh, I did. Business is going well over there, but there are still a few loose ends I have to tie up here and in New York. You know how it is."

"I can only imagine. Relocating your headquarters must be complex."

"It is, but the move has been a good one. So you're still in Seattle?"

"Rain or shine."

Jerry nods. "That's a good spot for you, though."

As they talk, Dominic pumps his finger in and out of me in a steady, unforgiving rhythm. My hands shake as they grasp at his jacket, which barely hides our dirty little deed.

I can feel my body responding against his delicious finger, my pleasure blossoming. I'm so close to falling apart in front of this stranger. If I wanted to, I could clamp my thighs together and stop Dominic from finger-fucking me into oblivion. I could join the conversation and shoot a well-deserved dirty glare at him for putting me in such an embarrassing situation. I could do all of that.

But I don't.

Finally, he and Jerry wrap up with promises of getting lunch before we depart for Seattle.

Dominic turns back to me, his face now a mask of pure lust. His finger slides out of me with a slick pull, and I nearly gasp at the loss.

"Let's go."

I step down from the bar stool with quivering limbs. I'm following close behind him, my cheeks flushed and my brain fuzzy, confused and uncertain and still reeling from the immense pleasure he can make me feel.

What just happened? Why did I let that happen? Jesus, Presley, what line won't you let him cross?

In the elevator, Dominic doesn't touch me, he just stares straight ahead, watching the numbers change as the elevator climbs higher. He looks angry, and I have no idea what could have possibly set him off.

I want him to back me up against the wall so hard that the handrail makes an indentation in my ass. I want him to lay hot, open-mouthed kisses against my throat while he cups my breasts and grinds his leg between mine.

But he doesn't do any of that. Instead, he stands a foot away from me, quiet and seemingly uninterested. I feel like I'm back on the plane with the man who wouldn't so much as acknowledge my presence.

Meanwhile, I'm still trying to catch my goddamn breath.

What the hell is this?

Once the suite door is closed behind us, Dominic finally touches me again. But it's not the kind of touch I like. It's harsh. Unfeeling.

He pulls at the zipper of my dress, yanking it off me in a few ungraceful motions. The fabric bites at my skin as it leaves my body, and suddenly I'm completely naked before him. With one hand, he grasps my breast, and the other he dips between my legs again—

But this time I stop him. I take one step back, and another. When he follows, I place a firm hand against his chest.

"Stop." My voice shakes but I'm not afraid.

No. I'm fucking *furious*.

Dominic stands before me, his eyes dark and his chest heaving with labored breath. Yes, he's turned on. Probably even more so than I am . . . *or was*. But he stills at my command.

"Stop?" he asks, his voice filled with questions.

I stand my ground. This little game he's playing will not be on his terms.

It's going to be on mine.

CHAPTER NINE

Dominic

"Stop." Presley's voice trembles, and her hand presses firmly against my chest.

Taken aback, I drop my hands immediately.

We freeze together in the dark, panting. I'm burning up; I've undressed her already, only her lacy black bra remains, and I ache to finish the job. I could feel that she wanted me when I touched her at the bar. So, why is she calling a time-out?

I'm the one who should be pissed off—not her. One touch, and she has me losing all control.

I flip on the light so I can meet her eyes while she explains herself. "Are you going to have a hard time following instructions on this trip?" I ask, my voice still low and husky with the desire she so abruptly blocked.

Presley is flushed too, but she stares back defiantly. "I don't want you like this. This version of you . . ."

"I'm no different than I've been all along. This is the real me."

"Bullshit. I know you well enough by now." Her expression is serious, and I have no idea what I've done to anger her.

"What do you know about me, Presley?" I ask, cocking my head as I watch her.

She swallows, gathering her courage. "You're not this man. This hard, unfeeling, dominating . . ."

I place one hand against her cheek, caressing her skin, and Presley leans into my touch.

The truth is, I don't know who I am anymore. Before Presley, my life was a series of well-orchestrated details. Commute. Work. Home. More work. The occasional fuck session to blow off some steam. She's turned everything upside down—all in a matter of weeks. Who could blame me for trying to get back some of the control?

Presley swallows, still watching me with wide eyes, waiting to see which version of me she'll get next. "You aren't this man, Dominic. I've seen it

. . . when you let me in," she whispers, wrapping my hand in her much smaller one.

"What do you want from me?" My voice is more anguished than I intended, and I inhale deeply, trying to calm my raging heart.

"You. Just you."

"I'm here, aren't I? I'm trying."

She nods, her eyes finding mine. "I am too."

"What do you need?"

She wets her lips with her tongue, watching me. "Kiss me."

I realize she's right. We broke up, and then I had my fingers up her dress before we'd even officially made up—before we'd even kissed. Sometimes I forget how young she is, how inexperienced, and how much of a dominating prick I can be.

Using two fingers, I tilt her chin up and press my lips softly to hers. "That better?" I murmur, my lips still brushing hers.

She reaches up, curling her fingers in the hair at the back of my neck. "Yes. More."

We kiss again, slower this time, deeper. Her rapid heartbeat flutters against my chest as my fingers work at undoing the clasp of her bra.

Everything in me strains toward her, screams to eliminate the distance between us. I want to forget every messy fucked-up thing and just lose myself in her. Instead, I correct her.

"I'm the boss, not you. We agreed that you wouldn't be the one in charge."

Except I was never in charge to begin with when it comes to her. Whenever I see her, I have to have her; if the slightest shadow passes over her face, I need to do whatever it takes to bring back her smile.

"I haven't forgotten that." Presley looks up and her bold blue eyes lock with mine. "I came to London, didn't I?"

I seize her mouth. The fire that's always simmering between us explodes—tongues writhe together, she moans against me, and I gasp for breath. I must be pressing her backward because suddenly we're on the bed, and her fingers are tearing at my buckle and shirt buttons like she can't get me bare fast enough.

Damn, this woman is dangerous. I've never known anyone who gets under my skin like her. My restraint has already frayed to a thread.

Deciding I need to take back control of this situation, before giving in to our unresolved lust becomes something far too intimate, I pull myself away, rising to my feet at the edge of the bed. Presley blinks up at me in confusion. She's mesmerizing, naked, and pink-cheeked with arousal, her lips plump and damp from our ferocious kisses, and I have to steel myself not to just dive back in.

"Enough of that," I say more gruffly than I feel. "I want you on your knees now."

She looks surprised for a moment before a mix of desire and determination comes over her face. She sinks gracefully to the floor at my feet.

"Very nice," I say, petting her hair. And I mean that. Maybe I shouldn't be praising her on a night that's supposed to be all about my needs, but she *is* a pretty sight, ready and waiting to serve me however I ask. "Take out my cock."

My shirt is already hanging open and my belt is God knows where, but I'm still going to enjoy watching her trembling fingers unzip my dress pants.

"That's it," I say, encouraging her when she wraps me in her warm fist.

She grips the base tight. My heart racing, I

watch her soft pink lips meet the tip of my cock. A loud groan of relief escapes me as they part to slide down over the shaft. It's been too damn long since I've had her. I'd forgotten how combustible we are together—how quickly I lose the battle for control when she's near.

She follows her hand up and down, sucking hard, her tongue lapping like she's missed this as much as I have. The sight of her is overwhelming. She sure as hell isn't new to sex anymore . . . she knows exactly what to do now.

Still, I can't let her just do whatever she pleases tonight. I tangle my fingers tight in her hair to direct her where to go, how fast to bob her head and work her sweet mouth. She lets out a soft murmur that burns in the pit of my stomach. I make a mental note that she's partial to a little hair-pulling, then remind myself for the millionth time that what she enjoys isn't what this trip is about.

"You look amazing like this." My voice comes out as a groan. I didn't mean to say that aloud, but it slipped out. Whatever. A little encouragement can't hurt, right? "I could watch you suck me all night."

She sighs and squirms, rubbing her thighs together. The thought that she's trying to ease her own arousal makes me throb.

But when I notice her free hand creeping between her legs, I say sharply, "I didn't say you could touch yourself. I'll give you your turn soon enough . . . right after I'm done fucking your mouth."

She makes a tiny noise that could be a whimper and moves her hand up to cup my balls.

Oh fuck. I won't last long if she keeps this up.

Sighing, I start slow, rocking my hips in shallow strokes. The head of my cock sliding over her tongue feels incredible. She adjusts quickly, keeping up her own work while letting me move her. I thrust faster, deeper—still careful not to gag her; I'm sure she doesn't know how to handle that yet—but taking my pleasure rather than letting her give it to me.

Blood roars through my ears and pulses in my cock. *Fuck*, this woman is the hottest thing I've ever seen. She looks up at me, her lashes fluttering, her lips still sealed around me, and suddenly I'm way closer to my own release than I planned to let myself get.

I pull her away, but she continues to stroke me, and my orgasm threatens. "Enough," I growl.

She snatches her hand away sheepishly.

I haul Presley to her feet and give her a quick, light slap on the butt. A startled squeak escapes her. "You almost made me come too soon."

"I'm s—"

I crush my mouth to hers, cutting her off. I'm going to devour her. Take all she can possibly give me.

Keeping my fingers knotted in the silky hair at the back of her neck, I slide my other hand down her body. She sucks in a sharp breath when I push two fingers into her; for the second time tonight I'm knuckles deep inside her. She's so wet, so perfectly ready for me. My thumb finds her swollen, eager bud and she arches, clutching at my back and shoulders like she's trying to hang on for dear life. But I want her to lose that control. To surrender everything to me.

I devour her mouth as her hips buck and stutter forward into my touch. I'm consumed by her scent, her sounds of pleasure, the feel of her under my hand.

Yes, this is exactly what I wanted tonight—for both of us to forget the past and the parts we're supposed to play. We're not boss and intern, or even lovers, because lovers have a shared history and complicated emotions I'd rather ignore. Tonight, we're just man and woman giving in to our mutual lust for each other.

Our kiss evolves into a messy clash of lips and tongues. She's moving into my hand now, writhing in my grip, and her begging cries grow louder and more urgent. Suddenly, she gives a desperate whine and her arms tighten so hard they tremble. My aching erection twitches up, straining. She's coming already.

"Dom . . ."

She groans and I kiss her deeply, possessively, as she spasms around my fingers in rhythmic waves. That's it. She's mine now. It's time to take what I've been needing but didn't let myself have since she broke my heart.

I keep rubbing, letting her cling to me until her quaking subsides. Then I withdraw, releasing her hair. Both of us are flushed, sweaty, panting from desire.

I pull out of her with a slick noise and can't resist bringing my hand up to taste her arousal. Her eyes lock onto my tongue running over my fingers. Then I press them to her lips, and she only hesitates a second before opening up to suck them. My cock bucks at the feel of her eager mouth closing around my fingers.

When she's done, I press a kiss to her forehead. "Get back up on the bed. On all fours this time."

She obeys with shaking knees, still out of breath. I admire the view—her pert ass raised up like an offering, and the needy spot between her legs glistening, ready for me.

Quickly, I open a condom and roll it on. I kneel behind her and drag my tip over her sensitive flesh, teasing her. She tries to thrust back, and my hands clamp down on her hips to hold her still. I'm the one who dictates when we start, and I'll dictate when we finish.

"Last chance to call this off." My voice is deep and rough with desire. It would just about kill me if she took that chance . . . but I'm almost certain she won't. "We aren't going to stop until I'm satisfied."

"Please," she says, so softly I almost miss it.

"Good girl." I bite the back of her neck and bury myself deep in her wet heat, trying to forget everything that happened between us before this moment.

It almost works.

CHAPTER TEN

Presley

Tonight has taken a turn I never could have imagined. I know I should guard my heart, that I shouldn't romanticize this moment, but it's too late. We move together perfectly, my soft pants punctuating the moment that has grown heavy with expectation.

His cuff links rest beside my earrings on the bedside table. Our laptop bags sit side by side on the floor near the desk. I have no idea what it all means, but something big, surely.

I feel so many warring emotions at once, it's hard to focus on them all. First, there's pleasure unlike any I've ever known. But more than that, there's relief at his forgiveness, and somehow too, I can also feel him releasing all the baggage of his past, excising it with precision as our bodies meld together.

Dominic fills me in a way I never could have imagined. He must feel it too, this powerful pull, because we release a simultaneous groan in the otherwise silent room.

He withdraws briefly, guiding me onto my back so he can hover over me. In this new position, I can see his eyes. I just wish his emotions were as easy to read as his pleasure.

His pupils are dilated and his lips part with a silent moan. He pushes in to the hilt, and I wrap my legs high around his hips, grinding myself closer.

"Uh . . . that's so good, baby." He groans, his voice deep.

I know by now not to read too much into the sweet endearment.

He moves in long and deep strokes. I'm still so sensitive from my earlier release that I have to dig my fingernails into his shoulders for stability. I can hear the sounds of our sex, a loud, wet slap of flesh against flesh. My breasts bounce with the efforts of his thrusts. I can't help but release quiet gasps every time I feel the tip of him hit that once mythical, now *very* real sweet spot inside me.

With every pump, I feel closer and closer to the man who has remained such an emotional anomaly to me. As I watch his sculpted body move over me, memories of our brief history flood my brain.

The moment when he picked me up on that horrible night, and the instant relief I felt just being near him.

The moment his gruff voice over the phone promised that I still had my job, and elation soared inside me.

The moment in his office when he told me he wanted me with him on this trip.

"Dom!"

When I cry out his name, he leans closer so our naked, sweaty chests are pressed together in an intimate embrace. He moves above me, taking everything I have to offer.

I comb my fingers through his thick, dark hair, gripping it in my fists. I can feel the goose bumps rise on the back of his neck. I can feel him coming close with every shaky breath he takes, and I love knowing that I'm the one bringing him to the brink.

With every nip at my neck, my earlobe, and my lips, I can feel the secret tenderness he tries so desperately to keep reined in. His thumb finds my center and rubs it in methodical circles, just how he knows I like. As I get closer and closer to the edge, my eyelids flutter closed and I brace myself for yet another fall into bliss.

And I am falling for him. Despite my best efforts, I have fallen.

When I tumble over the edge again, Dominic gathers me close, holding me against his chest as I tremble and gasp.

With his lips against my neck and a hand on my breast, Dominic releases a soft grunt, and his grip on me tightens as he finds his own release. The sound he's making—somewhere between a gasp and a groan—is like a drug. I would let him do anything to me just to hear that sound again.

When he's recovered, he lifts himself up, propped on his elbows over me. His eyes are hooded and his forehead is beaded with sweat. I hold his firm biceps in my shaking hands, rubbing my thumbs against the muscle with a tenderness I can hardly describe.

But in a blink, he's gone, both physically and mentally.

He climbs from the bed, removing himself

from my soft touch almost as fast as he ripped off my clothes. He walks across the room, tosses the used condom in the trash, and picks up his boxers, tugging them on. Then he grabs his laptop. He's already on his way into the living room of the suite when I find my voice.

"Where are you going?" I *hate* how vulnerable I sound.

"I have some work to do. You can go to bed without me."

And just like that, I'm alone.

What the hell?

Surely he felt it, the same things I did—the intimacy, the closeness, the intensity . . .

That's why he left. He's not ready to face it, to accept it, and I'll have to be okay with that . . . for now.

My body is still warm and flushed from the mind-blowing experience we just shared, but my heart is cold. I fight back the sting of tears, determined not to waste any time feeling sorry for myself. All I can muster is the will to wrap myself in the fluffy duvet and curl into a ball on the bed.

After I take a few deep breaths, my heart begins to slow. A voice in my mind that sounds a lot like my mother lulls me to sleep.

Just be true to yourself, Presley. Be true to what you want.

CHAPTER ELEVEN

Dominic

The next day, I come back to the hotel early. Well, right on time by normal standards, but I had to politely fend off a dozen offers of dinners, cocktails, anything that would keep me listening to pitches for another few hours. Not that I mind skipping out. I have a five-thirty date I wouldn't miss for the world.

When I enter the suite, Presley is on her laptop, her lips pursed in thought. Working, of course—both of us are always working. She looks up when she sees me, her lips curving into a grin.

I'm still not sure how I feel about what happened between us last night. I have the sense that I'm playing with fire and will most likely get burned.

But I return her smile, my lips twitching as I

take her in—with her black leggings and oversize sweater and messy bun. She looks every bit the college coed she was not long ago, and I'd be lying if I said that wasn't tempting as hell.

"How was your day, dear?" she teases.

I chuckle. "Just fine. Yours?"

"Same," she says cheerily.

There's a lot we need to talk about, but first I need to do something else. "Can I borrow the desk for an hour?"

"What?" She looks back at her laptop. "Oh, sure, no problem. I can use the bed."

I repress a quip about how we used the bed last night and it most certainly didn't involve working or checking email. Now isn't the time. And as today wore on, last night's events had started to . . . not sit right with me. But I don't have time to examine my selfish actions right now.

I pull out my own laptop, open up video chat, and call home. After a few rings, the faces of Lacey, Emilia, and Francine fill my screen.

"Daddy!" my girls cry ecstatically, and the sound of their loving voices calms the uncertainties inside me almost instantly.

"They've just had their breakfast," Francine informs me.

"What did you eat?" I ask.

"Poo-poo," Lacey stage-whispers, and they both collapse, giggling.

"Come on, you guys," I say, but my mouth twitches up despite myself. Their laughter is just too infectious to resist.

"Tell your papa what you *really* had," Francine says.

Emilia fidgets with the hem of her shirt. "Waffle and juice and, um—"

"Presley!" Lacey screams.

I glance back at a very startled Presley caught halfway across the room.

"Uh . . . forgot my power cord," she mumbles.

Now that Emilia has spotted her too, both girls are hollering her name over and over. Presley is watching me helplessly for some cue as to how to handle this explosion.

Francine fixes me with one of her patented looks. She has many looks that I've learned to read over the years since my girls were born, and this one ranks among the most powerful—the expression that says, *What the hell are you up to, Dom?*

Christ, all these women with their significant stares. I heave a sigh and relent. "Come say hi to them."

A tender smile spreads over Presley's face. I stand up to let her use the chair and lean over to one side, one hand on the desk, so I can still see the screen. Though I'm focused on Emilia and Lacey, I can't shake the awareness of how close Presley and I are and how good her hair smells.

"How are you two little monkeys?" Presley asks.

"Good-how-are-you," they chorus proudly.

Their twin bond is freakish sometimes. That whole finishing each other's sentences is real.

Presley grins in delight. "Wow, so polite. Did your daddy teach you that?"

Emilia shakes her head as Lacey chirps, "Franny."

Ouch. As if I needed another reminder that I'm never home to do anything with them.

Francine shoots me an apologetic look.

"I see. Nanny Franny is great, isn't she?" Presley asks.

There's little they love more than rhymes. The girls erupt into giggles and shouts of "Nanny Franny!" that restore the smiles to all our faces.

"Do you want to show them your picture?" Francine asks.

Emilia's eyes go huge. "Yeah!"

Francine holds up a sheet of construction paper covered with a chaos of circles, lines, and scribbles in all colors of the rainbow.

Presley glances at me, looking lost, and I hold back a snort. It's not her fault she hasn't had as much practice as I have interpreting their drawings.

"What a cool dog," I say. "And I like how big that tree is."

Presley catches on right away. "I love dogs. Did you see all this neat stuff at the park?"

"We petted him," Emilia replies. "Doggies say *bark.*"

"They lick people because they don't know how to kiss right," Lacey explains with a very solemn expression. "I know everything."

Presley laughs, which gets them so excited that they start yelling over each other and it's impossible to understand.

"You have to take turns talking," I remind them.

They settle down only slightly, but I can't bring myself to quash their energy further. It's impossible not to smile while watching them chatter on, telling stories of the park that segue into the books Francine has read them before bed.

It's astounding how attached to Presley they are, considering she spent about half an hour with them over a week ago. They clamored for her like she's as important as their uncle Oliver.

I should be a little jealous of Presley apparently being a more interesting video chat partner than their own dad. But somehow, talking to them together with her feels . . . natural. Yet again the memory surfaces of Presley sitting at my table, entertaining my girls, like we were all a family. Like that was how things were supposed to be.

I shake away the thought.

The hour flies past, and all too soon, Francine says gently, "Time for us to go bye-bye."

The girls look unhappy about this, but they

both dutifully say, "Good-bye, Daddy. I love you." Then they astonish everyone by adding, "Love you, Presley."

Presley and I look at each other in surprise for a moment before she replies, "We love you too."

"I wish I could hug you two right now." I swallow a growing lump of emotion. "I'll save them all up and you'll get so, so many hugs when I'm home, okay?"

"Okay."

"Promise!"

I end the call and step back to let Presley get up, stretching out the stiffness from standing so long bent over. She's still wearing such a soft, sweet smile, and before I know it, I'm launching into my half-formed plan.

"Listen, um . . . would you be interested in going out to dinner?"

"Oh, sure. I'll change into something nice." Presley starts rooting through her suitcase. "Who's coming? Other than Roger and his wife, of course. What was her name again?"

"Monica. But actually, uh, it'll be just us tonight." I spent most of the day with Roger, and there's only so much of his company I can take.

She straightens up to blink at me.

I pull my hand down over my mouth. I knew this conversation would be awkward, and yet it's somehow even worse than I predicted. "I . . . wanted to take you out to apologize for how I acted last night."

She watches me without moving. "For which part?"

I eye her. She can't genuinely not know, right? With time today to reflect on it all, I know I acted like a dick. The odds are high that she's testing me. But I guess it's only fair for her to want a more detailed apology.

"How I treated you. I touched you in public without asking first. I didn't kiss you until you put your foot down. I played rough. I didn't hold you afterward, even though I could tell you wanted physical contact." I sigh, raking a hand through my hair. "Sometimes I forget that I'm the only man you've ever slept with."

She cocks her head, a faint line appearing between her brows. "What does that mean?"

"You know . . . you're inexperienced. With a

woman who's been around the block, it's more okay to play a little fast and loose, because she knows what she likes and doesn't like, and she won't be afraid to call a time-out."

"But I *did* tell you to stop," she fires back, crossing her arms over her chest. "Doesn't that prove I'm capable of holding my own?"

I would laugh at her trademark resolve if I weren't rapidly approaching exasperation. "I'm trying to apologize for not treating you better."

"I know. And I appreciate that. I just need to know you see me as an equal. I don't want you handling me with kid gloves. I agreed to this"— she waves a hand as she searches for a word— "arrangement of my own free will."

"Even a casual partner still deserves to be treated right."

She nods slowly, like she's confused over my choice in words.

I tip my head toward the celling and draw a deep breath before meeting her eyes again. "So, would you like to go to dinner with me?"

She stares back at me for a moment before softening. "Yes. That sounds really nice." Her expression turns the tiniest bit mischievous. "But it's still not a date, right?"

I keep a poker face. "Right."

"Just wanted to make sure. I'll get dressed," she says, then heads into the bathroom to get ready.

I should feel better having gotten that apology out of the way, but somehow I don't. I only feel more confused.

• • •

Overlooking the Thames, we share platters of native Cornish oysters on the half shell and roasted vegetables and a variety of desserts.

Although we're talking shop, analyzing the various offers I've received over the past two days, it doesn't feel at all like work. It's easy and fun, and highlights all the aspects of this job that get my blood pumping.

Presley is so sharp, and we tune so easily into each other's wavelengths that our collaborating feels effortless. It's nice. Relaxing, even. With a business partner like her, synergy isn't just a marketing buzzword, but something real and invigorating.

I'll start bringing her to meetings soon, I decide. I was a fool to ever think of restricting her to my bed—she's too valuable an asset to be kept away from the negotiation table.

The cocktails and conversation loosen my tongue until I'm rambling about my most unlikely dreams. "Someday we'll be worldwide." I smile, taking the last sip of my wine. "An Aspen property in every country—or at least one on every continent, I'll settle for that."

Presley smiles at me over her glass of prosecco. "Even Antarctica?"

I realize I misspoke, but I go with the flow and joke, "Sure, why the hell not? An ice palace with attached ski resort."

"And penguin-watching tours," she says with a giggle.

It feels good to see her laugh, to laugh together with her. When was the last time I felt so good? Probably right before I found that fucking Genesis stuff in her bag. The worst of that is behind us now . . . but still, I can't deny it was a useful wake-up call, pulling us apart before we got too entangled. Too invested in a connection that could never last.

I sigh, the reality of my life bringing me back

down to earth. "On the other hand, I really need to start trimming back my hours. I shouldn't miss *all* of Emilia and Lacey's childhood." That was meant to be another joke, but it came out downright dismal.

"You can do both, right? If you find good people to delegate to," Presley says.

I rub my chin. "Maybe. Easier said than done, but maybe."

"Your kids are so cute . . . *I* want to spend more time with them, and I'm not even their parent." She gets a weird look on her face. "Sorry, I don't mean to overstep my bounds or tell you what you should do or anything."

"I didn't take it that way. What about you? How's your family?" She rarely mentions her father—one of the many things we have in common—but she lights up beautifully when the topic lands on her brother.

"Michael is doing really well at school. He loves his classes, and . . ." She giggles. "He keeps talking about this guy. Every time we talk, it's *Elijah said this*, *Elijah did that*, or *oh my gosh, Elijah's so cool*."

I chuckle. "Are they dating?"

"If Michael ever works up the courage to ask him out, we just might see." Toying with her last bite of dessert, she asks way too casually, "Speaking of relationships . . . do you think you'll ever be looking for more?"

She's challenging me. Like she always does. "I don't see how I could fit any more obligations into my already limited schedule."

As soon as the words are out, I wonder why I avoided the question instead of just saying, *No, I'm not looking for some big romantic love affair*. For some reason, I'm reluctant to shut her down cold. Even though I really should, because there's no way anything beyond sex can happen between us.

It just wouldn't be sustainable. She's so young and has so much ahead of her. I'm jaded and overworked, and am barely getting by with the two ladies who need more of my time than I have to give at the moment. It would be foolish of me to pretend we could make it work.

"We could always ask the cards for solutions." She taps her purse.

"We don't need to go to that extreme. I can see the future just fine. Us, twenty minutes from now, getting naked back in our hotel room . . ."

Presley meets my eyes and nods, but there's something conflicted in her expression.

• • •

As soon as our door clicks shut behind us, I sweep her up, kissing her fiercely. My fingers find the zipper at the nape of her neck. I pull it down and let her elegant evening dress pool on the floor, revealing a satiny black bra with matching panties. I growl appreciatively and push my hips forward so she can feel what she does to me.

"You're stunning," I murmur.

Her breath hitches. "How do you want me?" she whispers against my mouth.

Well, if she's in the mood to challenge me, I know a way to challenge her right back—something that will also ensure we avoid a repeat of last night.

"Tell me what *you* want."

She blinks up at me. "I thought you liked being in control, boss man."

"I'm changing the rules. You're in charge tonight. Think you can handle that?"

Her brow furrows for a moment as she thinks. Then she starts opening my shirt, her delicate fingers working button by button. She stands on tiptoe to slide it back over my shoulders until I can shrug it off. Next comes my belt, which she sets neatly on a nearby chair before unzipping my pants. She's so methodical, I'm amused watching her.

When I'm bare, she nudges me. "Lie back on the bed, Mr. Aspen."

I do as she says, enjoying the view as she strips off her bra and panties while never breaking eye contact. No words are spoken as she straddles me, rolling her hips to spread her slickness over my erection—and *damn*, she's already wet and ready. Well, that makes two of us. My cock aches for her to get on with it and ride me already.

But a niggling thought at the back of my mind tells me that it won't be that cut and dried.

CHAPTER TWELVE
Presley

"**G**et over here and ride me," he murmurs, his hand sliding up until he finds my breast and gives my nipple a playful pinch. Pleasure zings through me, both at his words and the feel of his hands toying with my breasts.

Tucking my legs on either side of his torso, I raise up on my knees and position myself over him. Dominic lets out a soft groan, shuddering as I lower myself.

"Fuck," he grunts. "Don't move for a sec," he says as his hands tighten on my hips.

My eyes sink closed at the exquisitely full feeling of him inside me.

When I open my eyes, Dominic's hooded gaze latches onto mine, and his expression is filled with things I've never seen before—wonder and vulnerability, and of course enough pleasure to end this ride in about three minutes flat if we're not careful.

His hands find my ass and he lifts me, easing out and then sliding me back down again. We both groan. With his help, I find my rhythm, riding him as we gaze at each other. I plant my hands firmly against his chest, and Dominic rocks beneath me.

His hand slides to my throat so that his thumb can find its destination—my mouth. I suck it in, relishing the taste of his salt and my own sweat. Then he drops his damp thumb between my legs, and I whimper at the immense sensations shooting through me.

With each caress, I lose track of the rhythm of my hips, growing more and more erratic with my thrusts. Suddenly, unexpectedly, my orgasm washes over me in a powerful wave. I curl into his chest, rocking with pleasure. With one hand tangled in my hair and the other gripping my ass, Dominic thrusts hard and fast into me, his own orgasm right there.

When it's all over, he cradles my still trembling body against his chest. His fingers play with my hair as his breathing slows.

I don't want to jinx it . . . but I think we're cuddling. And I'm pretty damn sure he's allowing it.

I bury my nose in his neck, breathing him in and stretching my long legs against his until we're tangled together. And then, to make matters worse, I feel the soft press of his lips on the top of my head: a kiss with no expectations. Just tenderness.

Damn. I squeeze my eyes closed. I'm falling so hard for you, you confusing-as-hell man.

I don't want to think about the repercussions of that just yet. Instead, I welcome a deep, uninterrupted sleep wrapped in his strong arms.

• • •

The rest of our time in London is everything I wanted it to be. I sit in private meetings with him, now invited as a special guest. I consult with him after, weighing options and crunching numbers over mug after mug of tea.

I've learned more in four days of business boot camp than I did during four years of college, reading every textbook on the subject. On top of that, I've been exposed to how business works in a foreign country, specifically one known for its hotel industry. Being at Dominic's side, I have access to every brilliant mind in the business.

We also have sex. Lots and lots of sex. An insane amount of sex. In our bed, in the shower, once in the massive tub, against the vanity . . . it really doesn't take much to get him riled up.

Or me, for that matter. His sexual appetite turns me on, if I'm being honest. As soon as I see his eyes go dark and his lips part, I know exactly what his thoughts are. And he knows mine.

Knowing Dominic in this way has been so incredibly fulfilling. Sure, it's just sex. That's what Bianca would say. Yet I can't help but feel the protective layer of my heart dissolve, allowing admiration to unfurl and blossom into honest affection. In those quiet moments between the soft kisses and dozing in his arms, I feel like I have a damn good chance at knowing all of him.

As long as he'll let me.

• • •

Okay. I put the cart ahead of the horse again.

The hum of the plane's engine would normally calm me, but I'm rigid and anxious. As soon as we boarded, I sensed yet another mood swing in Dominic. His profile is hard and cold as he types away at his laptop, utterly ignoring my presence. He's back to business as usual, treating me as he would any colleague at work.

"I've got some emails to send," he said as soon as he sat down. Before I could ask him what I could help with, he popped in his earbuds. *Nice*.

I order some wine from the flight attendant. His moodiness is getting really, *really* aggravating. Just this morning, we were fucking each other's brains out in bed, literally one flesh. Now I've been given the millennial equivalent of *talk to the hand*.

I take a sip of my rosé, not at all caring that it's early afternoon and hardly drinking hours. If I'm going to be yanked around like this, I'm going to need a little liquid courage.

What if I really like him? What does that mean for me? It's not like I could suddenly squeeze into his life. He has zero time for another human being. And even if he did, he would be extremely particular about his choice in a partner. He has two children to raise, after all.

The mere thought of stepping into the role of *mother* makes me feel ill. I'm so young. I'm not ready to raise children. I barely consider myself an adult yet, and it's been hard enough for me to help Michael out.

I have no idea what I'm doing, and Dominic certainly isn't giving me any clues.

Well, that decides it. What happened in London will just have to stay in London. If he's going to be cold and detached, then so will I. It's better for my work anyway. I can finally utilize the tools I've acquired and actually make something of myself.

I can focus on me.

CHAPTER THIRTEEN
Presley

"You look stressed," Michael says in lieu of a hello, kissing my cheek.

"Thanks?" I shake my head. "That for me?"

He nods at the coffee on the table and slides it closer to me while I take a seat across from him. "I hope you're not stressing about the money again, sis, because—"

I shake my head. "No, nothing like that." To be honest, I'm always worried about money, but for once, something else is occupying more of my brain space than the dwindling balance in my checking account. "Actually, I'm having some guy troubles."

"Yeah?" Michael says, watching me curiously. I have no idea why, but I realize we've never discussed things like this before. "You know that happens to be my specialty, right?"

"Guys?" I ask, grinning at him.

He nods, satisfied with himself. "If it's got a dick, I can help. Lay it on me."

"Michael . . ." I chuckle, taking a sip of my coffee.

I haven't seen him in a few weeks, but after arriving home from London late last night, his was the first number I called. I slide over the small magnet I got him from the hotel gift shop, and he lifts it in his palm, eyeing it curiously.

"What's this?"

"A little souvenir. It made me think of you." I shrug.

Michael's lips twitch. "I love it, but you're not going to get out of talking about this. Seriously. Tell me. What seems to be the problem?"

I take a deep breath and release it slowly, debating on where to start. Surely I can't admit to my little brother the entire messy extent of what's gone down between Dominic and me. Can I?

"It's a little complicated," I say, stalling for time and picking at the label on the paper cup.

"It always is." He sighs.

"Guys suck sometimes."

He nods. "That we do." He slips the magnet into his bag and waits for me to continue.

"I just . . . I feel like everything has spiraled out of control with the guy I've been seeing. He's older—only by a few years, but he has two kids."

Michael's eyes widen.

"I know. He's a single dad. But that's not the part that's causing issues. His little girls are amazing, actually. But he . . ." I put my face in my hands. "I can't believe I'm about to admit this to my little brother."

"Out with it."

I grin, somehow amused at seeing this grown-up side to him. "He wanted to keep things casual," I say with an eyebrow wiggle, hoping Michael can read between the lines so I don't have to admit the extent of my debauchery—and with my boss, no less.

"Ah. The good old fuck buddy who swears he doesn't want something serious."

"Yes!"

"Happens all the time," he says sadly.

"So, what am I supposed to do? Call him on it? Demand he change?"

Michael frowns, shaking his head. "Nope. That would only backfire."

I figured as much. And I don't want to put more pressure on Dominic. His life is filled with it already. I want him to choose me because he wants me. Just like I want him.

"So, what am I supposed to do?" I ask.

Without missing a beat, Michael leans forward. "Take Jude my freshman year, for example."

My eyes widen. "You slept with Jude? I didn't even know he was gay."

He shrugs, waving me off. "I don't think Jude knows he's gay. But yeah, even if he didn't want to admit that to himself or even take one step out of that closet, he wanted me. And I gave him what he wanted. But once we slept together, that was it. He ghosted me and pretended it never happened."

I make a face. "Jeez, Michael. I don't know if I want to hear about your sex life in vivid detail."

He purses his lips. "Don't be such a baby. It's

not a big deal. And not everyone remains a virgin until they're eighty-two, Miss Priss."

I roll my eyes at him. "I was twenty-two, not eighty-two, you ass."

"Still," he says. "This is an area I know a lot more about than you do. So, do you want my advice or not?"

I sigh in resignation. My little brother is right. "Okay. Yeah, I do. Sorry for overreacting. I need the advice, because honestly, everything I've tried has failed."

Michael smiles. "Tell me what you've tried."

"Well . . . I've tried being the casual friend with benefits he says he wants. I've tried putting myself out there more, pushing him a bit, connecting with his little girls to show him we could be more too. Neither of those worked."

He nods, his expression turning happy. "Duh. Of course it didn't work."

I narrow my gaze. "Then why do you look so happy?"

Grinning, he drums his fingers on the table. "Because I know exactly what you need to do."

My brows push together. "Well, are you going to fill me in or what?"

Michael pats the back of my hand. "Oh, I'm gonna do more than fill you in. I'm going to make sure you have that man eating out of the palm of your hand."

I laugh for the first time all day. It feels damn good.

Then I listen aptly as Michael describes the best strategy, nodding at his sheer genius.

I only hope he's right, because I don't know how much longer I can take this back-and-forth with Dominic.

• • •

Jet lag is a major drag. I never really understood that until last night. I tossed and turned for hours before slipping into a fitful sleep.

After coming to the decision that I have to put my career first, I decide I can't let these little setbacks affect me. I roust myself out of bed, power down two cups of scalding-hot coffee, and make my way to work like it's my job.

It is your job, Presley. Wow, I must be tired.

The *click-click* of my heels on the office floor is a familiar sound. Yes, this is what I need—a consistent and predictable work environment in which I can be the best version of myself. Not an undefined relationship with a man whose mood changes so dramatically that I wonder if he's really two people. The first, a charming, funny, considerate man. The other, a loathsome asshole with no consideration for the feelings of others.

No, I don't have time to juggle my work and a man who can't decide who he is. *I'm still figuring out who I am.*

My determined stride across the office falters as I spot Jordan, packing his personal items away into a box. *Why?*

"Jordan!"

"Oh, hey, Prez," he says in his usual chipper way. But his dimpled smile doesn't reach his big blue eyes.

"What's going on?"

"The internship is over. The others already packed up. I guess no one got the job."

I feel as though I've been dropped into the cold, dark ocean. Like the plane I disembarked just yesterday hadn't landed safely at all, but rather had crashed right into the tumultuous sea.

"You'd better get packing too." Jordan hands me an empty box, then turns back to his almost empty desk, once covered in his alma mater's insignia, pictures of his dog, and an assortment of bobblehead dolls. "It's reassuring to have Bill Gates and Elon Musk nodding at me in approval all day," he said to me back in our first week.

Tears prick my eyes. "Jordan . . ."

"Oh, Prez, don't worry. We're going to be fine. You're practically a genius, so you'll get a paying job in no time. And who can resist this face?" He smiles with his eyes this time, showing off his full, brilliant grin.

I wish I could return the enthusiasm, but all I can manage is a sad half smile and a reluctant nod.

On my way back to my desk, the *click-click* of my heels sounds less like a battle cry and more like the cheap knock-off shoes that I bought in college. They've been glued back together so many times . . . if the heel snapped off one of them today, I wouldn't even be surprised. *A fitting end.*

Back at my desk, I start collecting my own things. I don't have much—a Brown insignia pin, a picture of Michael, a stained coffee mug, some miscellaneous business books, and a preserved sticky note my mother wrote for me back in middle school. I LOVE MY SMART GIRL! it reads in a splash of blue marker. She tucked it away in my lunch box the day of a dreaded geometry test that I'd been studying for all week.

I caress the worn paper, and for a moment consider throwing it in the trash. *Smarts can only get me so far, Mom.* But if I'm anything, it's sentimental. I can't throw this piece of my mother away.

One by one, the pieces of me go into the box, which gets heavier with every memory. *Just like my heart.*

"Oh, you're here already?"

I squeeze my eyes closed. I'd recognize that voice underwater if I had to.

Dominic stands behind me, probably leaning against the empty desk kitty-corner to mine that once belonged to Jenny.

I refuse to turn around. *He doesn't deserve my attention,* the bitter little girl in me insists. Even as angry as I am, I know how immature that is.

"I am," I say over my shoulder.

"I see you're already moving out."

"I am."

"Good."

I want to scream in his face, but I restrain myself. For as much of a stress nightmare this internship was at times, I wouldn't have changed the experience I gained for the world. I learned more here than I did in four years in college. I'm grateful for that.

"Thank you for—" I murmur, but Dominic is already walking away.

I take a deep breath and turn around quickly, not letting my gaze linger on the broadness of his shoulders, and head straight for the elevator. I maneuver the box against my hip so I can press the DOWN button. The elevator dings and Oliver steps out.

"Whoa, where are you going?"

"I'm going home. Thank you so much for helping me acclimate—"

"Wait, Presley. Why are you going home? Are you sick?"

I don't understand. Is this some sort of trick?

I'm so gullible . . . I can never tell.

"I was let go," I say carefully. "All the interns were let go."

"Not you," he says with a smile. "You've been selected."

"Selected?"

"Didn't Dom tell you?"

"No," I practically shout. *Rein it in, Presley.* "Dominic doesn't tell me anything."

"That doesn't really change over time." Oliver sighs, smirking. "But you'll have plenty of opportunities to get to know him better as our new director of operations."

My heart skips a beat. He can't be serious. "Director . . ."

"You've been promoted. Congratulations." Oliver turns and points down the hall to a small office. The door is ajar. If I squint, I can read DIRECTOR OF OPERATIONS in bold print on the placard. "That's your shiny new office."

I'm speechless. I must really be wearing a funny expression, because Oliver can't keep it together. He laughs like I've told him the best joke he's heard all year.

"Go put your stuff down. And then go see Dom. He'll tell you about his decision. And your salary," he says, poking me playfully in the arm.

I practically run to the little office. It is gorgeous—small but somehow feeling expansive with its tall window overlooking the cityscape. I slide my box of all-things-Presley onto the glass surface of the desk (*my desk!*) and wander around the room. It's so pristine . . . so cozy.

I can imagine early mornings, sipping coffee at this desk while scrolling through emails. Bright afternoons, leaning against this window, making calls to clients. Late nights curled up on the love seat, jotting down important things to do the next day in my planner. Joy threatens to overwhelm me, but I have something to deal with first.

I stride purposefully across the office, ignoring the heads turning to watch me march toward my boss's office. When I open the door without knocking, he's staring out his own window, his hand on the glass.

He turns, surprised. The light catches his eyelashes and casts dark shadows across his cheekbones. I'm almost dazzled by his beauty.

Almost.

"I thought I was being let go," I say. It isn't a question, but I need answers.

His eyes squint, an almost comical expression of confusion on his face. I would laugh, but I'm too . . . pissed? Surprised? In shock?

"Jordan was packing," I say, quieter now.

"The interns were let go. You're not an intern anymore."

I flush as Dominic takes slow steps toward me. "But you saw me packing up my desk."

"I thought you were moving into your new office. Do you like it?"

"Yes," I say in a small voice. "But no one told me."

"I'm sorry. I thought Oliver caught you when you walked in. I shouldn't have assumed," he says in a voice so tender, I almost look over my shoulder to see if his daughters are here.

"It's okay. I just didn't know what was going to happen to me."

"You should have known," he says with a teasing smile. "Your work as an intern excelled above all the others. You're diligent, adaptable, bright."

With every compliment, he takes a step closer to me. Leaning way too close, he reaches over my shoulder and pushes the door closed.

As soon as it clicks shut, his hand settles on my waist and his lips brush against mine. The kiss is so warm, so precious. I feel cherished and irreplaceable with every caress of his thumb against my cheek, even if I know that's not the case. When he releases me, I'm breathless.

"How will this work?" I ask, looking into his dark eyes for reassurance. "Won't the others find it unprofessional? I don't think they'll take me seriously if—"

I stop myself as Michael's words of advice ring through my head. I can't fall for his charms. I can't keep sleeping with him. I need to be firm. It's the only way. Too bad it's nearly impossible because this man turns me into a pile of goo with one smoldering look.

"Let me worry about that," Dominic murmurs, his lips still inches from mine and his palm on my hip. I don't realize I'm shaking until I put my hands on his chest, not pushing him away, but not letting him come any closer either. "Don't you want to know what your salary is?"

I pull back to look him in the eyes. "Well, duh."

He chuckles, and my body shakes with his. I join in, until we're both laughing a little too loudly. He kisses me once more on the lips before taking my hand and spinning me around like we're dancing. Suddenly, I'm back at the door.

"Go talk to HR. They're waiting for you."

"Thank you, Dominic," I whisper. I know he can feel my gratitude by the way he smiles and shoos me away. *This man can't handle too much emotion at once.*

When I get to the human resources office and sit with my coworkers Daniel and Brienne (*oh my God, coworkers!*), the reality of the situation finally sinks in. I'm about to take over an entire department of Seattle's Aspen Hotels, including a team of two assistants to do my bidding and a salary that makes me choke on my coffee.

"Seriously?" I ask, still coughing.

Daniel and Brienne laugh and confirm the number. I can see their mouths moving, but I can barely hear them over the pounding of my heart. *They can't be paying me that much!*

"Congratulations, Presley," Daniel says, clapping his hands together. Brienne joins in the applause, and I wipe a pesky tear from my cheek.

I can hardly process the rest of what they tell me—something about a medical plan, stock options, paid vacation time, and a retirement account. Taking one more deep breath, I nod to everything they say, knowing I'll have to dig into the details later when I can think clearly.

"Thank you again," I say, rising to my feet, and they both smile at me.

Out in the hall, I dial my brother's number with shaking fingers. I get his voice mail. He's most likely at class. It doesn't matter—I can barely speak anyway. In a low voice, I leave him a quick and jumbled message to share the good news, punctuated with an "I love you!" at the end.

Once I'm back in my office, I shut my door and call Bianca. She answers immediately.

"Hey, babe, what's up? You okay?"

"Oh my God, Bianca."

"Oh my God, what?"

"I got the job."

Bianca screams so loudly, I have to pull the phone away from my ear.

"Yes, you did, bitch! Yes! You! Did!"

Bianca is so excited, my heart finally explodes. I jump up and down and squeal as quietly as I can. I'm still at the office, after all.

"It's insane! Oh my God! I can't believe it!"

"You better believe it! How much are they paying you?"

"Uh . . ." I laugh, almost drunkenly. "A lot."

"Yes! I guess that means you're buying tonight. We're going out!"

When we hang up, I allow myself one more excited giggle before I put my game face back on. I've got to get through several more hours before the celebrating begins. How I'm going to stay focused is beyond me, but I'm excited to get to work. I haven't been this happy in a long time. Maybe ever.

And there's so much more to come.

CHAPTER FOURTEEN

Dominic

I'm working late, trying to get through the last of today's urgent decisions so I can start with fresh business in the morning, when my phone buzzes.

"Yes, Francine, I know I shouldn't live at the office," I mutter as I grab my phone and look down at the screen.

But to my surprise, it's a text from Presley. And even more surprising, it reads: *heeyyyy sexxxy,* followed by a smattering of eggplant and fire emojis. *What the hell?*

I do a double-take to confirm that the sender really is her. Maybe someone took her phone as a prank? Then I remember that she got her promotion today, and text back:

I take it you're having a night out
to celebrate?

The response is immediate:

im so drink haha

I snort, my lips twitching. I've seen her tipsy before, but drunk is new. Getting to glimpse this new, uninhibited side of a woman who's normally always so disciplined is . . . charming.

I can tell. I'm glad you're having
a good time—you've earned it.

thank you soooo much I love you

My heart skips a beat. *She doesn't really mean that.* It's just the kind of thing people say when they're drunk.

come celebrate with me

You should enjoy partying without
your boss hanging around.

but you're why im here

I was losing my shit and this
promotion saved my whole entire
life

I really owe you

No you don't. You got the job because you were the best worker. It
                        was all you.

what if I wanna owe you? ;)

I'm not sure how to answer that, and in the
thirty seconds I spend deliberating, she adds something that makes me forget whatever I'd been planning to say.

I could let you do whatever you
want with my body

Holy shit. What I'd like to say is "I'm on my
way," but instead I type:

I'll ask if you still want that

```
                    when you're sober.
```

She replies:

```
boo :( at least dance with me.
```

I consider it. Francine is home with the girls, and I probably already missed my chance to kiss them good night anyway. I'm too burned out to make any more headway on work tonight . . . so, why the hell not? It would give me the chance to check up on Presley and make sure she has a safe way to get home. Plus, a drink might relax me a bit.

```
Sure, sounds like fun. Where should
                        I meet you?
```

• • •

Ten minutes later, I'm taking a ticket from the valet at the address she texted me. It's just around the corner from our office, and I can't help but notice it's the same bar where I first asked her to play my pretend girlfriend.

So much has changed since then, it's strange to think about.

In barely any time at all, we've gone from acting out an illusion to being real lovers. Or I guess I should say *fuck buddies*, since neither of us can afford to fall in love, but applying that word to Presley makes me frown. It implies something crass and shallow, and she means more to me than that.

As I enter, I barely have a chance to scan the place for Presley before she's flung herself out of her seat and into my arms.

"You came!" She's still wearing her work outfit and smells slightly of alcohol.

I return her hug and reply with a fond smile. "I said I would, didn't I?"

The woman who was sitting next to Presley walks around their table to me. "You must be the big boss man," she says, extending a violet-nailed hand. "I'm Bianca, Presley's roommate."

I shake her hand. "It's nice to meet you. I'm Dominic."

She grins, the corners of her eyes crinkling. "I've been dying to meet the famous Mr. Aspen. Presley has told me *so* much about you." Her impish, knowing tone has me wondering exactly what Presley might have told her.

I look instead at the table cluttered with empty glasses. "You guys really didn't waste any time. It's only eight o'clock."

"We met up right after work. Pres wanted to make sure she could leave early enough to get up on time tomorrow." Bianca shrugs with an expression of fond amusement. "At least, that was what she said about three or four cocktails ago. Now she wants to live here."

I chuckle, my gaze wandering back to Presley.

"Come dance!" Presley insists, tugging at my arm.

I let her drag me out onto the floor as a thumping beat starts playing. She loops her arms around my neck, I rest my hands on her hips, and that's where anything recognizable as "dancing" ends. Her wild side steps, shimmies, and sashays don't remotely match the rhythm of the song. Every time she lifts a foot, I can feel her wobble, and my hands on her hips steady her.

I guess it's reasonable that Drunk Presley isn't the world's greatest dancer. Not that I mind at all; she more than makes up for her lack of coordination with exuberance, and it makes me smile just to have her close. I chuckle and do my best to sway along with her erratic moves.

Then I gasp, because she's pushed her hips forward, writhing against my body. Before I can say anything, she spins around and enthusiastically grinds her ass onto my burgeoning erection.

I bite back a groan of need. *Damn*, when she wants something, no force on earth can stop her.

Someone whistles at us. It might be Bianca, but I have no idea, because Presley is totally intent on making my head spin with want. Giving in, I let myself caress her curves and nip at the tender skin at the back of her neck, feeling her pulse flutter under my lips.

"Behave," I say on a groan.

She pouts. "Tomorrow. Tomorrow I'll behave." Then she moves my hand over her breast and squeezes hard.

I growl into her ear, soft so no one else can hear, but forceful enough that she makes a throaty, desperate noise. When the song ends, she turns to me, her eyes smoldering with erotic promise . . .

. . . and then she trips. I catch her before she kisses the floor instead of me.

"Okay, I think it's time to go," I grunt out, then

call to Bianca, "Can I drive Presley home?"

"Fine with me. I was planning to leave with my guy." Bianca looks over toward a guy seated in the booth nursing a beer, then pats Presley on her flushed cheek. "Just make sure to text me when you get home, okay, babe?"

Presley flashes her an unsteady thumbs-up.

I give my ticket to the valet and wait with her at the front doors until it arrives, then escort her outside and into the passenger seat. She drapes herself over me as soon as I've slid into the driver's seat and shut the door.

"Sorry, guess I had too much," she mumbles into my ear.

"Don't worry about it. You're highly entertaining and educational." For instance, I've learned tonight that copious amounts of alcohol make Presley extremely silly and touchy-feely. The surprises never end.

She pouts. "Are you laughing at me?"

"You're tough enough to take it." I peck her on the cheek.

She shakes her head, now smiling at me.

The drive to Presley's apartment takes less than twenty minutes, and then I'm helping her up the front steps and inside.

I head to the kitchen and retrieve a bottle of water from the fridge for her. "Here. Drink this. You need to sober up."

She smirks at me, accepting the water bottle. "Yes, Dad."

I can't help but chuckle. "I am a dad."

Presley laughs harder. "You sure are, and an extremely hot dad. You're like a DILF."

Shaking my head, I laugh with her.

She finishes her water and meets my eyes. "Thank you for everything."

I'm assuming she means the promotion, but as I told her before, she earned it.

"And for coming to my rescue tonight," she adds with a nod.

"You're very welcome. Should we get you to bed? Where's your room?"

She nods toward the couch. "We're in it."

The tan sofa is ancient looking and sags in the

middle. A thin cotton blanket is draped over the back of it, and a pillow is shoved into one corner.

I frown. "You sleep on a couch?"

Presley waves her hand. "Yes, and don't look so scandalized, Mr. CEO. Keep in mind that until today, I was working full-time in an unpaid position."

"I guess that's true."

The fact that our internships are unpaid has never bothered me before now. Mostly because I've never considered what that means, or the sacrifices people would have to make. One of those sacrifices—at least in Presley's case—being a bed, or any real privacy.

She heads into the bathroom, and I hear her brushing her teeth. Deciding to make myself useful, I make up her bed for her, draping the white sheet I find folded on the coffee table across the sofa, and lay out her blanket and pillow. If there's one domestic thing I'm good at, it's tucking someone into bed.

Presley emerges with her shirt unbuttoned down the front and her hair wild around her shoulders. I watch as she strips off her work clothes and then help her tug an oversize T-shirt over her head.

She's still a little unsteady, and I don't know why, but I find her drunken state oddly adorable.

I place my hands on her hips and help her across the room.

"I can't have sex with you tonight," she says, giving me an exaggerated wink once we reach the couch.

"Okay . . ." I'm somewhat taken aback since I didn't plan on sleeping with her while she was in this . . . *state*, but still, I'm surprised she just blurted that out.

I have no idea if she's about to tell me she's on her period, or maybe that she's too drunk for sex, which I would agree with, but instead Presley nods.

"Sex confuses things between us. Doesn't it, Dom?"

I don't answer. Instead, I let her lean on me as she adjusts the blankets to her liking while I turn that question over in my head.

Barefoot and dressed in a T-shirt that nearly reaches her knees, she looks smaller, and even more innocent somehow. "You won't buy the cow if you're already getting the milk for free," she says quietly.

What in the world?

"Okay," I say, clapping my hands together once. "On that precious note, I'd say it's time for bed."

With my help, Presley sinks down into the soft cushions.

"You okay?" I ask, studying her in the dim light.

She lets out a huge yawn, nodding. "Just tired."

I should have asked if she's eaten, but I guess now's not the time. The best thing for her will be just to sleep this off. And besides, I really do need to get home.

As I sit on the edge beside her, she sighs drowsily.

"You're so good to me."

Am I, though? The small, guilty tightness in the pit of my stomach points to *no*.

"Taking care of you is the least I can do," I reply, not knowing if I'm even doing that much. Maybe I'm good *to* her, treating her right the best I know how, but I'm definitely not good *for* her. Yet I keep finding myself getting more and more entangled.

"You're good," she insists again, the words so quiet and slurred with impending sleep that I can barely decipher them.

"I'm glad you think so."

I stroke her cheek, and she lets out a sleepy *mmnn* noise. After pressing a gentle, chaste kiss to her forehead, I pull back and see that her eyes are already closed.

Stroking her hair one last time, I murmur, "Don't fall in love with me, okay?"

She doesn't reply. I'm not sure if she's fallen asleep or just not answering me. Then again, I don't really know whether I was talking to her in the first place, or maybe to myself.

I tug the blanket up over her and rise to my feet while so many unanswered questions dance through my head.

CHAPTER FIFTEEN

Dominic

The next day, Oliver and I drive out to check on the progress of several new properties scattered across Washington State. By Friday noon, we've made our way to Spokane and stopped for lunch at a pub the locals swear has the state's best pizza. After debating, we agreed that wasn't quite true, but they were pretty damn close.

We could have planned something more efficient than a multiday road trip, I suppose, but I don't often get to hang out with my best friend someplace that's not the office or my daughters' tea parties. And if I'm being totally honest, I also wanted a chance to clear my head and figure shit out about Presley, which is hard to do when I see her all day, every day, at work.

"What do you think of the town?" I ask, draining the last of my wheat ale. If this place has one thing going for it, it's the incredible beer.

Oliver shrugs cheerfully. "Seems pretty nice. It's no Seattle, but then again, I'm biased. With the airport and all the basketball tourism, I think our new location will get more than enough traffic to remain profitable, even with the first hotel already there. Especially since the cheap real estate keeps our expenses low."

"I see someone read the projections report."

He scoffs, pretending to be offended. "I'll have you know I always read everything I'm supposed to." Then his smile slips a bit. "Listen, can I ask you something?"

Oliver almost never sounds this serious. It instantly makes me suspicious.

"That depends on what it is."

"I need you to be completely honest with me here, dude."

"Christ, just spit it out."

He presses his lips into a flat line, breathing out through his nose, then asks, "Are you doing anything with Presley that you shouldn't be?"

I hope he can't see my shoulders tense. "You've already asked me that."

"I know," he says mildly. "It's not illegal to ask the same question twice."

"Well, the answer is no," I lie.

"Are you sure that's the story you're sticking with? I know you want her."

"What is it with you and this topic?" I snap. "Why are you so obsessed with the idea of me fucking her? How many times are you going to grill me about it?"

He sets his pint glass down a little too hard and a few drops of beer slosh out. "Dammit, Dom, don't lie to me. I'm your best friend—some would say your only friend—"

"Hey," I grunt.

"—and your vice president, so I need to know whether anything is happening that might fuck up things between our CEO and our new director of operations."

Oliver and the rest of my executive staff knew Presley was the right intern for the position, so I don't think he believes I offered her the job simply because I'm tangled up with her. I wasn't even the one who recommended her for the spot initially. The others had seen her work, and there was really no question. The rest of the interns did fine, but *fine* doesn't win you a midlevel position with a hefty salary and loads of responsibility. Presley was the only candidate who ranked high enough to meet our stringent criteria.

But he remains quiet, waiting me out, and in his stare is a stern warning. "She's a good girl, Dom. The kind of girl who will want a house in the suburbs with a dog and a lawn and a white picket fence someday. You couldn't give her that fairy-tale ending, even if you wanted to."

His words cut unexpectedly deep. "What, I'm not good enough to be Prince Charming?" *Shit*, I should have kept denying it. Getting offended only proves his hunch.

"Don't get your panties in a knot. I'm just being realistic here—you and she don't want the same things in life. Or at least not when it comes to relationships." His mouth quirks. "You're two of a kind when it comes to cutting a swath at work, though."

A heavy sigh escapes me. "I know," I mutter.

Believe me, I'm all too aware that I'm wrong

for her, and it's not fair to let her wait a single second longer on something that's never going to happen.

Too bad knowing that fact still doesn't help me stay away from her. When it comes to her, I'm utterly helpless. The more time I spend with her, the more my doubts and fears creep in, but the harder it is to pull away. Why can't I find the willpower to get my shit together?

"So, will you promise that you won't hurt her?" Oliver asks.

I wet my lips. "I . . ."

I have no idea how I'm going to finish that sentence, and I'm grateful to be interrupted by my phone ringing.

I'm much less grateful when I see it's Francine.

She knows Emilia and Lacey's daily routine and all their likes and dislikes—probably better than I do, I hate to admit—so it's rare for her to have a question. Usually, she can handle the unexpected without breaking a sweat.

"What's up, Fran?"

"Dominic!" Her voice is frantic and . . . weak?

My blood pressure spikes at the sound of toddlers crying in the background.

"Lacey threw up her morning snack. I didn't call you because I figured it was just the tummy bug that's been going around, it'll pass in twenty-four hours with no harm done, and you know me, I'm not afraid of a little mess, so I cleaned it up and put Lacey to bed with some Pedialyte and tried to calm down Emilia, but then suddenly I felt *awful*, and now I can't—"

"It's okay, Francine. I can come home. I'll be there as soon as I can." Which won't be very soon at all, seeing as Seattle is almost three hundred goddamn miles away.

"What's wrong?" Oliver asks, his brow creased.

I cover the receiver to quickly mutter, "Everyone in the entire world caught the stomach flu."

"—so sorry to call you back home," Francine is saying, "when you're out of town like this."

"It's okay, Francine. It's no trouble at all. But it'll take me a few hours."

I hang up and yank on my jacket. Of course this has to happen when I'm on the other side of the fucking state. Guess I should be thankful the virus waited until I got back from London.

"Sorry to take the car and ditch you here," I tell Oliver. "I'd fly, but by the time any seats became available—"

Oliver waves me off amiably. "No worries, man. I'll do the site visit and rent a car to come back tomorrow morning like we'd planned."

"Thanks. I owe you a beer . . . no, a bottle of whiskey." I throw two twenties on the table for my half of lunch and then I'm out of there.

I speed back down the highway as fast as I dare. All I can think of is Francine being sick, struggling to take care of two hysterical toddlers, one of whom is puking and the other probably not far behind, for five whole hours—maybe even six if I hit traffic.

Normally, if he weren't also in the wrong city, I could ask Oliver to cover for me in this kind of situation. But there *is* one other person who's good with my kids, who's in town and could relieve Francine right away . . .

I hesitate, then chastise myself and call Presley's desk phone. As soon as she picks up, I frown. I'd kind of hoped she wouldn't answer, so I wouldn't have to put her in this position.

"Hey, it's Dominic."

"Hi," she says cautiously, like she's unsure why I'm calling. She knew I was going to be out of town for a few days.

"Can you do me a huge favor? I'm sorry to even ask this, but I didn't know who else to turn to. Lacey is sick and Francine got sick too, and I won't make it back until evening. Would you be willing to watch the kids so she can go home and get some rest?"

Presley sounds exhausted, but she doesn't even hesitate, God bless her. "Absolutely. I'll leave right away."

I let out a long breath weighted with all my stress. "Thank you so much. You're a lifesaver. I'll make sure you get overtime pay for the rest of your workday."

"Don't worry about that. It's a family emergency—of course I wouldn't leave you or the girls hung out to dry."

"Still, I really appreciate you going out of your way."

"You're welcome . . . anytime," she says, and I can picture her smile perfectly. "Have a safe drive.

I'll see you at your place tonight."

"Thank you for doing this," I say, navigating my car along the on-ramp to the highway.

"It's really not a problem. Don't worry, okay?"

"Okay. 'Bye."

I hang up, feeling five parts relief to one part disquiet. This is the kind of boundary blurring that made things complicated between us in the first place.

Even so, I can't let my weird, confusing relationship with Presley stop me from doing what my family needs. If she had said no, that would be one thing, but since she's in a position to help, I'll just deal with the awkwardness later.

CHAPTER SIXTEEN

Presley

After being let into the building by the security guard, I knock on Dominic's front door, armed with a bag of tried-and-true holistic medicine: electrolyte drinks, ginger ale, and saltine crackers. My mother always took such good care of us when we were sick, so I made sure to pick up the necessary ingredients for a settled stomach at the store before I arrived at Dominic's building.

When I was standing in the grocery store aisle, comparing prices, I remembered I don't have to worry as much about the cost anymore. I can afford to buy the organic stuff . . . something I've never done before. If I were buying for myself, I would have probably gone generic as usual. But for Dominic's girls? I got the best stuff I could find.

Francine answers the door when I arrive. She is

pale as a sheet and gives me a wan smile. "Hello, dear."

"Hi. I'm here to take over," I say with a sympathetic nod.

"I hoped as much." Sighing, she looks positively exhausted as she opens the door and leads me down the hall. "I'm not feeling well myself. I should get home and rest before I make matters worse here. Dominic won't be happy to find both his girls and an old lady green in the face when he comes home."

"He just wants to make sure everyone is okay. Including you. Otherwise, he wouldn't have called me."

Fran gives me a look that says *I'm not so sure about that.*

I mean, why else would he have called me? I know where his apartment is, and he trusts me with his daughters. After thinking it through, I swallow. I guess that is kind of a big deal.

She smiles warmly at me before she picks up a large canvas bag and an umbrella and heads for the door. "They're resting in their room. There are sick buckets in the tub, just rinsed. Be careful not to touch anything you don't have to. Don't want you getting sick too, dear."

"Thank you, Fran. Please get some rest."

When the door closes behind her, I set down my bag and slip off my shoes. I tiptoe to the girls' room and peek my head inside. I don't want to wake them if they're sleep—

"Presley!" Lacey cries.

I guess they aren't sleeping.

The pale little girl tries to sit up in bed, but she's too weak and falls back into her pillow with a whimper. Emilia is almost unconscious, probably asleep until her sister's outburst. Her lips move but her eyes remain closed.

When I get closer, I can hear her saying, "Daddy. Daddy," and my heart aches. I didn't know Emilia was sick too.

This really is a ruthlessly contagious bug. I wonder if I should call Dominic and tell him . . . but he's driving and I shouldn't distress him any more than he is. I've only ever seen him frantic when it came to his daughters' well-being. I decide that he can find out when he arrives later tonight.

"Hi, monkeys," I say softly, approaching their beds. I know I'm not supposed to touch them, but they need a little comfort. I brush the sweaty curls from their faces and hold their hands.

"Where is Daddy?" Emilia asks, her eyes heavy with sleep.

"He's on his way. I'm going to take care of you two for a little while before he gets here, okay?" I know I'm a poor substitute for their father, but I hope I can at least provide them some comfort.

"Okay," Lacey whispers. "Can we play?"

I chuckle. "When you're both feeling better, we can play all you want. But until then, we've got to rest, okay?"

"But I'm thirsty." Lacey whines, squeezing my hand.

"You can have just a little bit of water. Not too much."

For the next hour, I alternate between the girls, relying on the memory of my own mother taking care of Michael and me. I give them each a few sips of water, even though Lacey is eager to guzzle more. I want to make sure they can keep this down before I give them too much.

Inevitably, when they start to feel sick again, I race to the bathroom to get the sick buckets. I barely get back in time for Emilia to lose the little bit of water that was in her stomach. She's so scared of throwing up that she shakes after every bout. I use a washcloth to wipe her mouth and then kiss her on the forehead, promising that it will all be over soon.

Then, when it's Lacey's turn to get sick, I try to help her through it, but she's a little more resilient than Emilia. It honestly amazes me how chatty she still is. When her head isn't in a bucket, she's asking me questions.

"Are you and Daddy married?"

"No, we're not married. We're just good friends." *Well, that's a very G-rated way of putting it.* I'm not about to tell his kids that I have no idea how to define my relationship with Dominic.

"How come?"

"Because . . ."

Luckily, Emilia throws up again before I have to come up with an answer. I brush her hair out of her face and help her blow her nose.

"I want Daddy." She cries, breaking down.

I know Dominic is still far away, at least three more hours by car. Knowing him, he's probably speeding here as fast as he can, traffic laws be damned.

"Let's wait for Daddy, okay?"

I gently lift Emilia from the bathroom floor and carry her across the hall. She's so light . . . even lighter with nothing in her stomach. I lay her down on her bed, and then check on her sister. With a fresh washcloth, I wipe the sweat from their faces and pull the covers up to their chins.

It really is alarming how contagious stomach flu can be. Ever since I first touched the girls, I've felt off. My own stomach churns at the thought of eating anything, even though I'm starving.

Oh shit.

• • •

"Presley."

When I wake up, I'm curled up on the floor at the foot of Lacey's bed with my head resting on a stuffed teddy bear. I must have fallen asleep after the girls did. The room spins, so I screw my eyes shut again.

Dominic stands over me and places a hand on my forehead. "You're burning up."

"The girls," I mumble.

"They're fast asleep," he says, looking over at their beds.

I sit up to see for myself, regretting it immediately. A rush of vomit rises, and when a bucket suddenly appears in my face, I let loose.

God. I haven't thrown up since the first time I drank in college. I'd forgotten how awful the sensation is. Like being punched in the gut and drowned at the same time.

"I'm so sorry," I mumble, wiping my mouth with the back of my hand.

Dom disappears and comes back in seconds with a wet cloth and a glass of cold water. He wipes my mouth just like I did for his daughters. His eyes are filled with turmoil, and his expression is stark. I stare at him, soaking up every second of this tender moment.

"Here, take a sip," he says.

I take the glass from his hands and sip. The water slides down my throat with the promise to come right back up later. *Yep, not doing that again.*

After taking the glass out of my hands, he carefully lifts me from the floor and carries me toward his bedroom.

I shake my head. "Just let me stay with them. I already have it. I don't want to infect your room too."

He doesn't say anything, doesn't even pause in his strides. He just keeps carrying me down the hall until we reach the master bedroom.

He sets me down on the edge of his massive bed. "You'll stay in here."

"But what about the guest room?" I ask.

"You'll stay in here," he says again, more firmly this time.

I nod, feeling dizzy.

Dominic pauses, appraising me as I slump over the edge of the bed. "Do you want to change into something more comfortable?"

When he glances at the jeans I'd quickly changed into before coming, I nod, realizing he's right.

"Let me find something that might fit," he says, already heading toward his massive walk-in closet.

After returning with a pair of cashmere sweatpants and a white cotton T-shirt, Dominic helps me remove my clothes—which is a good thing because my limbs feel so heavy that I doubt I could maneuver out of them on my own, and slides the soft cotton over my skin.

He turns his back while I unhook my bra and fish it out through the sleeve of the shirt. Then he gathers my clothes and takes them to the closet.

When he comes back to me, he holds a glass of water to my lips again. "A little more."

I groan, but I know he's right. I have to stay hydrated. I can't act like a toddler when he has two *actual* toddlers sleeping in the other room. I drink some more, but the room flip-flops, and I sink back into the bed with a groan.

He sits down next to me, careful to put a little distance between us. I'm grateful for it. If he gets any closer, I'll probably cling to him, and then there won't be anyone left to take care of the sick people.

"It's okay," he says, reading my expression. "I juiced up with some vitamin C packs on the way here."

"Yeah?" I ask weakly.

"Yeah. I'm going to be fine. I'm invincible." He grins.

I feel like laughing, but I know the effort would likely make me vomit again. I've already done that once in front of the most attractive man I've ever met . . . I could do without a second round.

Surprising me, he lies down next to me. "Thank you for being here," he says softly in my ear.

I can't bear to turn and look at him for fear of losing any more of my goddamn breakfast in his beautiful face. "Some help I've been," I groan.

I should have listened to Fran and not touched the girls. But the looks on their faces when I first arrived . . . they were so scared and tired. I had to show them that they would be taken care of.

"They're fast asleep and their fevers have broken. You've been more than helpful," he murmurs.

I can feel his gaze glued to my face. I'm flushed and damp with sweat, but not in the sexy *fuck me* kind of way. I don't feel self-conscious, though. I feel safe.

"I should thank you for being here," I mutter, my eyes sinking closed.

"You're welcome."

Was that a kiss I felt on my temple?

Dom, you can't tell me not to fall in love with you and then be like . . . this. You can't expect me not to feel anything for the man who has given me the world, from a ridiculous salary when I'm at my best, to tiny sips of water when I'm at my worst.

You can't expect that, because I'm already in love . . .

With a man who isn't capable of returning my feelings.

CHAPTER SEVENTEEN

Dominic

I'm woken up by two tiny, adorable heathens climbing on me and demanding pancakes. Part of me wants to be annoyed, wants to roll over and keep sleeping, or maybe chastise them for waking me up by climbing on me. Instead, there's a smile on my lips even before my eyes open.

Presley isn't far behind them, her hair wet from the shower, looking so much better than she did yesterday. When I ask how she feels, she admits she's starving too.

Surprised, but grateful to see them all bright-eyed and bushy-tailed again, I cook up a full breakfast, pour orange juice, and brew coffee. My three former "patients" wolf down their breakfast like they haven't eaten in days. I enjoy mine at a much more leisurely pace, but I'm sympathetic; a diet of broth, crackers, and bananas is hardly satisfying. I'm thankful it's Saturday and I don't have to rush off to the office once they're finally feeling better.

Now they're watching TV while I rinse our cups and syrup-smeared plates and load them into the dishwasher. Shutting its door, I ask Presley, "Want more coffee while I'm up? There's at least a cup left in the pot."

"Yes, please," she says emphatically. "I've missed it."

"After one single caffeine-free day? I'm pretty sure based on those parameters alone, that makes you an addict," I tease, bringing the pot to her proffered mug.

"Hey, it's no fun dealing with a wicked withdrawal headache on top of the flu." She takes a long sip with a happy sigh. "Ah . . . my hero. Thank you."

I'm not sure what's changed between us, but it's obvious something has. When I saw her sick and sleeping on the floor at the foot of Lacey's bed, something inside me shifted. And I can feel it now too. We're more comfortable together, more in sync than we have been. What started as a chemical thing—a lustful attraction—has given way to more, despite all my best efforts.

"I'm bored," Lacey says with a pout.

"Outside?" Emilia asks excitedly.

I don't blame them for being restless after a day stuck in bed. "Sure, let's go out and do something fun. How's the park sound?" It's not exactly an adventure, but I'm reluctant to go too far in case they aren't totally recovered.

When girls cheer, Presley laughs. "Looks like it's unanimous."

We pack a picnic lunch and get everyone dressed. "How about we take some stuff to feed the ducks too?" I suggest. As expected, I'm met with enthusiastic shouts, so I grab the rest of the loaf we used to make peanut butter and jelly sandwiches.

"No, bread is bad for ducks," Presley says. "I read somewhere that it's like junk food—it doesn't have the right nutrients—and it makes the water dirty."

I blink. "Really? I had no idea. What foods are good?"

"Um, let me check." She taps at her phone for a minute before saying, "Whole grains, veggies, stuff like that."

"Always doing research, even on your days off," I say, amused.

She shrugs with a self-deprecating chuckle. "What can I say? Ducks are important."

Emilia nods forcefully, and Lacey says, "Don't hurt ducks."

"You're all absolutely right. We should never hurt animals, and that includes giving them bad food," I tell them both before turning back to Presley. "I wasn't making fun of you—well, maybe I was, but that habit is also one of the things I lo—" I swallow the forbidden L-word just in time. "One of your many impressive qualities."

The hell was that? I sound like I'm giving an employee performance review.

Trying to get back to the sweet spot between dangerously intimate and bizarrely stiff, I say, "You seem to know at least a little bit about everything, and you always put in the effort to double-check and be totally sure of the facts."

"Oh . . . thank you." She gazes up at me, and her confused look makes something inside my chest ache.

Way to be an asshole, Dom, when she's here

helping you.

I take a deep breath and try to clear my head. Having her so close, here in my home, helping with my daughters, is seriously messing with me—although the last thing I want to do is send her away.

After some rummaging through the fridge and pantry, we assemble a mixed bag of oats, corn, peas, and lettuce. Then we head out on the short walk to the park, Presley holding Lacey's hand and me holding Emilia's.

At the park, we spread our blanket at the top of a grassy hill and set out our picnic. My antsy girls want to run off right away to feed the ducks, but I say, "Eat your lunch first, then you can go play." They inhale their PB&J sandwiches as fast as they can before scampering downhill toward the pond.

"They sure have a lot of energy. If I didn't know better, I'd have no idea they were lying in bed barfing all day yesterday." I blow out a relieved sigh. "I'm glad you all recovered so fast. Guess I should have believed Francine when she said it would only last twenty-four hours."

"It's still not fair that you never caught it at all," Presley says.

"My deepest apologies. Next time, I promise

I'll get sick as a dog and you can spend a whole weekend bringing me tea and soup and cleaning up my vomit."

"I'm gonna hold you to that." She playfully grabs my bicep and gives it a squeeze, then looks self-conscious. "Sorry, I didn't think. We shouldn't be doing stuff like that in public."

"It's all right." I can't bring myself to get too worked up about it. Warmed by the sun, listening to the trees rustle in the breeze and my daughters' giggles . . . I'm too relaxed to really be bothered by anything. I reach out to squeeze Presley just to prove how okay it is.

She lets her head rest on my shoulder, so I leave my arm draped around her. Together, we watch my girls play.

Lacey chucks as much food as her little hands can hold into the pond, drawing an army of gabbling waterfowl. Emilia takes a different approach, trying to tempt the ducks closer by holding out a small amount or dropping it at her feet. Whenever one approaches, she squeals in delight, startling it away, but it always returns.

When the sun begins to sink, I call to the girls, "Time to go home!"

"Awww," they whine.

"The ducks will still be here tomorrow. Besides, aren't you getting hungry?"

They look at each other, then reluctantly nod and walk over.

Back at the apartment, I put on cartoons to keep the little ones out from underfoot while we cook dinner. I check the pantry. We don't have a ton of options, since I've been too busy nursemaiding three people to shop.

Presley, peeking over my shoulder, asks me, "What are we going to make? I'm not a super-experienced cook . . ."

"Neither am I. They can be picky sometimes, but for the most part, they're good eaters." I'm still rooting around in the cabinets.

"Hmm . . . when Dad was working late, I used to make cheesy rice for me and Michael."

"That sounds promising. How do you make it?"

"It's mostly self-explanatory—boil a bunch of rice, dump in cheese and salted butter and whatever random veggies we had on hand, and stir it up." She checks the freezer. "Corn and broccoli will work great. And we can set some rice aside for rice pudding."

I make an uncertain noise. "They're not the biggest fans of broccoli."

"Covering it in cheese might change their opinion."

I shrug. "Fair enough. Let's do it."

I've never cooked as a team before, but it turns out to be surprisingly effortless. I babysit the two saucepans of rice while Presley microwaves the vegetables and preps the other ingredients so I can add them at the right times. We're a well-oiled machine, humming along at peak efficiency, moving around the kitchen without even bumping into each other.

In less than half an hour, we're finished. Still working in perfect tandem, we put the full plates on the table, help the girls into their booster seats, and clean up drips and messy faces between taking bites of our own dinners.

When dessert has disappeared and I start to see droopy eyelids, I say, "Uh-oh, somebody looks sleepy."

"Am not," Lacey tries to insist before an enormous yawn cuts her off.

Emilia gives us her most potent puppy-dog look. "One more TV? Pleeease?"

I get up to clear the dishes. "Sorry, I don't make the rules."

"Yes, you do," both girls chorus.

"Oh no, they've become too smart. We're doomed." I throw up my hands with a mock look of terror.

Presley giggles. "What's their usual bedtime routine? I was too wiped out to keep track of what you were doing while I was sick."

I tick off items on my fingers. "Bath, change into jammies, braid their hair, tuck them in, read them a story."

"I haven't braided anyone's hair since middle school," Presley says with a small smile.

"Okay, girls, you know the drill." I clap my hands. "Let's get cleaned up."

We corral them toward the bathroom with only a minimal amount of grumbling. Presley fetches washcloths and fills the tub with warm water while I undress the girls, and we share the task of brushing out their hair. Naturally, as soon as they get their hands on the bath toys, all complaints cease. Lacey is so intent on her windup swimming penguin that she barely notices anything I'm doing, even wiping her face. Presley washes Emilia while she scribbles all over the tub's walls with bath crayons.

In no time at all, we're at the last phase. "Close face," I say.

The two of them giggle and scrunch their faces as tight as possible. I quickly shampoo and rinse Lacey's hair. After a moment of confusion, Presley does the same with Emilia.

I check the clock. *Divide and conquer, indeed.* With the two of us working together, a task that normally takes half an hour is done in under ten minutes.

In their bedroom, we wrestle them into pajamas, careful to get their favorite colors right— green for Emilia, pink for Lacey. Presley sits on the bed with Emilia between her knees, but when I sit behind Lacey, she frowns.

"I want Presley braids!"

"Hey, you're hurting Daddy's feelings," Presley chides gently.

"Sorry," Lacey mutters, not very convincingly.

I chuckle. "Nah, it's okay. I do both girls' hair

nearly every night. I can go clean up the bathroom instead."

When I return from mopping up spilled water, setting out the toys to dry, and wiping crayon off porcelain, the sight of Presley stops me in my tracks. She's working on the last few inches of Lacey's braid with nimble fingers and a tender smile, humming under her breath. The scene is so cozy and serene. She looks . . . like home.

My chest aches, and my feet are stuck in their spot on the carpeting.

Presley glances up and smiles at me. "I'm almost done."

"Take your time," I manage to say, my voice tight with some unnamed emotion.

Maybe I'm only remembering what it felt like to have my own mother fuss over me—after the sun had gone down and I'd been scrubbed clean, lying on freshly laundered sheets while she combed her fingers through my hair and sang under her breath.

God, it was a lifetime ago. I'm a bit melancholy right now, thinking that the memories I have of being cared for by a mom won't be memories that my own daughters will ever have, and that makes me incredibly sad.

I squat in front of the girls' bookshelf, pondering, and take a deep breath. "What kind of story do you guys want tonight?"

"Make one up," Emilia says.

"With space aliens," Lacey adds.

"And princesses and magic."

"And ducks!"

"Hmm . . ." I rub my chin. "That's a lot of stuff. I'll need some time to figure out how to put them together." I come back to sit on the bed beside Presley and think.

In a couple of minutes, she's finished their braids. Once we tuck the girls in, I begin.

"Once upon a time, Princess Honey had a pet duck named Sparkle . . . uh, Bob. One day, Sparkle Bob said—"

"No, together!" Lacey says, interrupting.

It takes a moment to figure out what she means. Then I'm wondering how we're supposed to share a story and also make it up. I glance at Presley, smirking.

Her brow is furrowed. After a few moments, Presley says, "Sparkle Bob said, 'Let's go to outer space. I've always wanted to see the stars up close.' Honey agreed this was a great idea, so she traded her crown with a witch for a flying spell."

"Ducks fly," Emilia points out.

"But then Honey would be left behind, and he'd be lonely. And he'd get too tired if he tried to fly that far without magic."

I pick up the thread of the story before anyone can poke more holes in it. "They flew out into space, all the way to Neptune, and met the aliens that lived there. The aliens said, 'Great timing, we were just planning a party. But we—'"

"What kind?" Lacey asks.

Presley rescues me. "Jellyfish. They're giant purple jellyfish that float through the clouds like it's the ocean." She puts on a silly, squeaky falsetto. "And they talk like this."

Doing my best to imitate her pretend voice, I continue. "'But we don't have any good party snacks. Can you get us some cupcakes?' Honey and Sparkle Bob agreed to help. They flew back to Earth to make a thousand cupcakes, then returned to Neptune."

"They invited the witch too, since they couldn't

have done it without her," Presley adds.

"Right, of course. And they all had the best party ever. Many cupcakes were eaten. The end."

Lacey and Emilia's eyes have drifted closed and they're wearing contented smiles. When we're sure they're asleep, Presley and I tiptoe out into the hall, turning off the bedroom light behind us and silently shutting the door.

"You're amazing," I tell her in a hushed tone, our faces close.

"So are you. But, um . . . what is 'close face'?"

"Huh? Oh, that." I chuckle. "A while ago, I accidentally said 'close face' instead of 'close eyes,' and they thought it was hysterical. So I've been saying it at bath time ever since."

She stifles a giggle. "Aw, that's so cute."

I grin at her. "Seriously, though, you're a natural with the girls. They're crazy about you."

Presley turns her head slightly as if to hide the soft look in her eyes. "I'm glad—they're so much fun." Then, almost shyly, she steps closer to me. "We make a good team."

How true that is. It feels so natural to take care

of the household together. And watching her with the girls . . . it's like there's been a Presley-shaped hole in our family all along, and I just never knew until she stepped into it. Francine is great, but maybe the girls have been needing a woman in their life who's more like a mother than a nanny.

And right now, I can't deny that I'm in need too.

"Come here," I murmur, my voice husky.

Taking her face in my hands, I lean in for a thorough, smoldering kiss, rubbing my thumbs over her beautiful high cheekbones. With a moaning sigh, she presses close, wrapping her arms around my lower back. I indulge in our kiss for another minute before leading her down the hall to my room.

We draw together, all mouths and hands and desire, our clothes scattering over the floor. I sit back against the headboard, pulling her atop me to straddle my lap. This is only the third time I've had Presley in my bed. Once right before she hurt me, once after . . . but tonight is different. And any pain or doubt I felt before is gone.

"Are you okay with this?" I ask, wrapping her in my arms. I recall Presley's drunk declaration that she couldn't have sex with me because it only confused things between us. At the time, I kind of agreed, but now, I feel anything but confused.

"I want this," she says, circling her hips as she teases me.

I grab a condom and roll it on as our mouths stay fused together in a hot kiss.

As soon as I'm ready, she sinks down onto me and we moan together. The feel of skin against hot, sensitive skin is overwhelming, and I hold her close while she finds her rhythm.

She rides me, slow yet so intense. I kiss her mouth and breasts, suck her nipples, nip her delicate earlobes, earning a beautiful gasp with each touch. I bury my face in the curve of her neck to leave gentle bites and feel her pulse racing under my lips and tongue. Presley's warmth and softness and sweet scent envelop me until nothing else exists. Until she's my whole world.

Deep within me, I know we're not fucking, but making love. I know we've gone far beyond anything I ever expected to exist between us. I know it means I'm weak. And foolish and completely out of line.

I just can't bring myself to care.

CHAPTER EIGHTEEN

Presley

I could kiss Dominic's neck all night. My tongue trails across the thick line of muscle, finding the vein that quivers when I nip on it . . . and from the sounds he's making, I think he'd let me kiss his neck all *week*. As we rock against each other with our limbs entwined, our lovemaking has elevated from awkward and ungraceful to positively divine.

Lovemaking. That's what this feels like.

His eyes are searing deep into mine, no longer a power play or a challenge to see who will look away first. Now our gaze feels like balance. It's like he's finally seeing something in me . . . something that he wants in his life.

Is that even possible? My heart surges with the idea.

He groans again and kisses me hard on the mouth, and my mind goes blank. Now experienced lovers, we coax each other over the edge of pleasure. There are no more games or teasing. We help each other get there with the assurance that there will be time later for games.

I shudder when I come, feeling my inner walls wrap and pull against him buried deep within me. I bite my lip, trying to hold back the scream that's perched on my tongue. It starts to escape as the orgasm intensifies.

"Shh, shh, shh."

He covers my mouth with his, and I moan loudly into his kiss, trembling.

His cock twitches inside me, making me quiver and arch my back. The clenching of my body is enough for him to lose control. I've grown greedy for the look on his face when he falls apart. His dark blue eyes sink closed, his brow furrows, and his full lips part.

"*Fuck*," he says on a breath.

The exhale after his orgasm is always shaky and hot against my neck. He lifts his head to meet my eyes and licks his lips. I smile down at him. He smiles back.

"What?"

"I'm just looking at you," I say, pushing his sweaty hair off of his forehead.

"Hmm." He hums, tucking my hair behind my ears. "And for how long are you going to look at me?"

"For as long as you'll let me."

I grin, then attack him with quick kisses, one on his nose, and one on each of his cheeks, his forehead, and his chin. He laughs as I turn his head this way and that to get the right angle.

Suddenly, he takes control, pulling us back onto the cool sheets. His arms are tight around me, his legs rubbing against mine. This time, we're most definitely cuddling. I whine when he moves away.

"I'll be back," he says with a laugh. "I just need to clean up."

He gestures to his dick, still sheathed in a condom and my slickness, and I blush. I never knew sex was so messy. Seeing my shyness, he leans in with a growl and bites me softly on the neck until I dissolve into laughter. When he comes back from the bathroom, he wraps me in his arms like he'd never left at all.

I would forsake all the pillows in the world if I could sleep on Dominic's chest every night.

Would it really be every night, though?

I'm too overcome with sleep to doubt myself further. With the scent of him all around me, and the feel of his strong arms holding me close, I drift off.

• • •

Thump, thump, thump, thump!

I wake with a start.

Thump, thump, thump, thump!

"What is that?" I ask, my eyes wide with panic.

Dominic is already out of bed, throwing on a shirt and pair of sweats. "Someone is knocking on my front door. Stay here."

Dread sinks into my skin like a cold rain. Who could be here at this hour? It's not even five o'clock in the morning. Fran would know better than to knock so loudly and wake the girls. I peek my head into the hall and hear murmuring voices.

What's going on?

I throw on one of Dominic's shirts, doing up the buttons as fast as my fingers will let me. I tiptoe into the hallway, past the girls' room, closing their door on the way, amazed that they must have slept through the pounding. *Thank God.*

When I get to the end of the hall and peek around the corner, I'm relieved to see Oliver.

"What's happening?" Dominic says in a stern voice.

Whatever this is, it seems serious. I should respect his privacy . . . but I need to know. I lean against the wall, just out of sight. Listening.

"You weren't answering your phone. I thought you'd want to know right away."

"Know what?"

"It's a media circus," Oliver says in a concerned tone I've never heard him use before. Usually, his voice is playful, or at least cheerful. "You have to turn on the news."

I hear the shuffling of feet and a soft click as Dom turns on the television. I peek my head around the corner, momentarily blinded by the brightness of the TV in the darkness of the room.

"Which channel?" he asks.

"All of them," Oliver says solemnly.

Dominic turns back to the screen. I squint to read the words, and my heart falls right out of my chest. The headline panning underneath the anchor's austere expression reads:

breaking news: ceo pays for sex. escort reveals all.

Oh my God.

"Presley," Oliver says.

I'm standing in clear view now, my eyes glued to the television. I don't even know when my feet carried me into the room, but Oliver's spotted me.

"Why are you . . ."

But I can't hear him. The anchors casually toss grenades back and forth with their words—phrases like "outed by an anonymous source" and "public shame" and "reputation on the line." I can barely make sense of it.

Dominic's face is angled away from me, and I look at him imploringly, unable to read him. I just want to know what terrible thoughts are running through his head right now. His body is pulled tight like a string, like he's about to snap.

Oliver sighs, pulling me out of my tunnel vision. When we make eye contact, he lets loose a strangled sort of laugh. "Well . . . this is awkward. Are you guys together?"

Dominic says, "No," at the same moment I say, "Yes."

My face flushes hot with emotion. *Well, that's humiliating.*

Oliver takes that as his cue to leave.

"I'll see you both at work." Before he closes the door behind him, he pauses. "Just let me know if I can help you, man."

The door clicks shut.

I take a shaky breath, processing everything that's just happened.

Help Dominic? The idea that Dominic would let anyone help him almost makes me laugh. If he could, Dominic would do everything himself. I don't know how he's going to get out of this shit show without the help of Oliver, his PR team, me . . .

"No."

The memory of Dominic's hollow answer to

Oliver's question about us resounds through me. Staring at the stony wall of his back, I finally comprehend the bitter reality of his feelings for me.

As much as he cares for me, for my body, or for my popularity with his daughters . . . he will never make room for me in his life. He has told me in so many different ways, so many different times over the past couple of months. Every time we had the chance to grow closer or shut the door on our issues, he chose to shut me out. I romanticized our relationship in my head, but the truth is, he neglected or completely ignored me more times than I can count.

Latent rage bubbles like lava beneath the surface of my calm, and my eyes flood with angry tears. You tried so hard, Presley. You've done everything you can for him. He's made it clear he doesn't want you. Are you going to go down with him too?

"Presley," he mutters, his voice hoarse, and I brace myself. "I—"

"TV?"

We both whip around to see Lacey rubbing her eyes sleepily. Over the sound of blood rushing in my ears, I didn't hear her tiny feet approaching.

My heart softens. She looks like a little angel in

her white pajamas and beautiful bedhead of messy curls. She yawns and scrunches her eyes closed, giving Dominic enough time to shut the TV off. It would be horrible for the girls to see their father like this, even though we both know they could neither read nor understand what's on the screen.

"No TV. Let's go back to bed," he says firmly. His voice is clear and calm, like he wasn't just about to break my heart into a million ugly pieces.

I can imagine exactly what he'd say. *I can't have more complications.* And he would be right. He has two daughters and an entire company to look out for in the wake of this tabloid drama.

He takes Lacey's little hand in his and turns her back toward her room.

"Emilia had bad dream," she tells him. "Booming. Was monster?"

Oh, so they did hear the door.

"No monsters out here. We should go check on your sister, hmm?"

Dom doesn't spare me a second glance as he lifts Lacey into his strong arms, his bare feet padding down the hall.

With every second I stand alone in his living

room, I feel pieces of myself disappear. I could very well be a ghost, haunting a future I'll never have.

I finally understand my place here—it isn't my place at all.

I walk down the hall, slipping past the family that will never be mine, and into his room. With shaking hands, I undo each button of the shirt I'm wearing, fold it carefully, and ceremoniously place it on the covers. I mentally say good-bye to the bed where I lost my virginity. When I take my things, there will be no trace of me left here.

I yank on the clothes I first dressed in thirty-six hours ago, grab my bag, and head for the door. As I pass the girls' room, I can hear Dominic's low voice promising them that he'll scare away all the monsters.

I don't even check to see if he looks through the doorway to catch me before I leave. I couldn't say no to him if he asked me to stay. Or worse, I couldn't handle it if he said nothing to me at all.

So I won't give him the chance.

CHAPTER NINETEEN

Presley

From the window next to this café table, the sky looks heavy with unfallen rain.

I pick at the torn edge of the menu as I wait for Michael to show up. He texted me that he'll be a few minutes late, so I probably should have taken my time coming here. I could have taken the scenic route from Bianca's apartment by the pond . . . *no.* I would just see the ducks and think about the girls. *And him.* And I desperately don't want to think about him.

I don't want to think about how Dominic's eyes light up when he looks at me, or his laugh when his girls do something silly, or the way he squeezes me tight against his chest when we're tangled in his bed. I especially don't want to think about my last memory of him: the cold silhouette of his back against the TV newscast that froze out any chance of our relationship amounting to something.

Did you really think that would happen? I scoff loud enough that a barista at the counter turns to look at me with an odd expression.

I dip my head down, pretending to clear my throat. So much for making this café my usual haunt. I'm practically one step away from talking to myself.

As I sip my coffee, it occurs to me that this is the very same café where I first met Austin. It was when Michael had asked me for more money and we sat across the room in the armchairs. I can even see the case where they keep the banana bread where we struck up our first conversation.

As for Austin . . . what a colossal disaster that turned out to be. My heart aches at the memory of Dominic's face when he found the Genesis folder in my bag. It was so hurtful that he thought so little of me, that he thought I would betray him and risk everything to help a presumptuous stranger.

But he did hear you out. He did forgive you.

I tell that annoying voice in my head to shut the hell up. Dominic also spoke to me like I meant nothing to him. He tossed money at me like I was a whore. And then I was so desperate for his forgiveness, I spent days afterward groveling.

No. I'm done making excuses for his behavior. I can't put more effort in than *he*—

When the menu tears in my hands, I swear under my breath and tuck it under the little succulent centerpiece, hoping no one noticed. Now I'm turning into a crazy person . . . sitting alone in a café, destroying private property and muttering to myself.

I stare out the window, watching the hustle and bustle of the street. With each passerby, I imagine what it would be like to be that person. The man walking his tiny round dog. The woman on her morning jog. The teenagers locking their bikes across the street. Simpler lives.

What would I trade for a life with fewer complications? I could do without the couch I've come to associate with a perpetually stiff neck, or I could trade in my homophobic father. Instead, I have a roller coaster of emotions inside me and a complicated relationship with a man I can't seem to say no to.

While all of these thoughts rattle in my brain, a tall iced coffee lands before me, followed by a handsome twenty-year-old.

"Hey, sis," Michael says, all smiles. He takes off his blue beanie with a sigh and leans back into his chair. His hair is a mess, and when I lay eyes on him, I smile for the first time all morning.

"Hey, crazy hair." Smiling, I reach over the table and pat the stray tufts down.

"I barely slept," Michael admits, looking up at me through his lashes as I attempt to finger-comb his bangs out of his eyes. "I didn't shower so I could sleep in."

"Ew, is this sex hair?" I grimace dramatically, wiping my hand on his shirt.

Michael shrugs with a cheeky grin. I'm glad someone is in a happy relationship.

"Is that promotion hair?" he asks.

I roll my eyes. I have my hair up in a messy bun, like it always is when I'm not working.

"Yep, this is my eighty-grand-a-year look." I smirk.

Michael's eyes go wide. "Whoa, really?"

"Thereabouts," I say. Is it inappropriate for me to share my salary with my struggling-artist brother? Before I can answer the question for myself,

Michael does.

"You are so cool. You . . . wow. You deserve that," he blurts, his eyes shining with emotion. "You've always deserved it. *Finally* someone sees that!"

"I'm not so sure," I mutter.

"What do you mean? Your boss must think you're the best if she gave you that salary."

"He. And no, I don't think he thinks I'm the 'best,'" I argue with aggressive air quotes.

Michael waits for me to continue, sipping on his iced coffee.

"He's a really complicated person," I say. "One minute I think I know what he wants, and the next I realize I'm completely wrong."

"That's annoying," Michael says.

That's one word for it. Can I tell him everything? I rub my thumb on the stains on my coffee cup.

Michael takes my hand. "Presley, are you okay?"

"Yeah, why?" I ask with a very unconvincing quaver in my voice. I have to be strong for Michael.

I can't break down in front of him.

"What's going on? What happened with that guy you were seeing? Did my advice help?"

I laugh, a tear escaping my eye and landing with a soft splash on my hand. *If only it were that simple.* "It's complicated."

"You said that. Come on, Presley. Tell me. We're the only family we've got," Michael pleads, his hand warm against mine.

I finally raise my eyes to his. "My boss is the guy I was seeing."

I can see the color drain from Michael's face. *Oh God, what have I done?*

"Did he hurt you?"

"No, no. Not like that. It was entirely my choice. As soon as I met him, I fell for him. If you knew him, you'd understand. He's so handsome, and he's really committed to his work and his family. And the way he speaks, it's so honest. I got to see it firsthand as his intern. So I fell for him. *Hard.* And I thought . . . well, I thought he was falling for me too." The words pour out of me as freely as my tears.

Michael hands me his napkin, and I blow my

nose wetly into the scratchy paper.

"If he didn't fall for you, he's an idiot. You're the best person I know," he says quietly. "You deserve someone who's gonna treat you right."

I smile weakly. Why can't everything be so simple?

"Are you going to keep the job? I can drop out, you know. I'll get a job at the club. I know they're looking for bartenders. Elijah says—"

"No. No way. You're not dropping out of school. I didn't get this job for you to up and quit," I say firmly, and Michael stares at me.

"Sorry," he says with a laugh. "You really sounded like Mom just then."

My heart aches. "I miss her."

"I miss her too. But I'm glad I have you," he says, every bit the sweet boy he's always been.

I couldn't live without him.

"What are you going to do about . . ." He trails off.

"Dominic."

"Ooh, Dom." Michael smirks. "Is he . . ."

like wildfire—destroying everything in its wake—including my reputation.

Gia called from the agency first thing that morning and told me she had deleted my file and that we needed to cut all ties. I told her that was fine. I don't plan on using her services again anyhow. But of course, the damage was already done.

• • •

By Wednesday, the story still hasn't died down, and it's starting to wear on me. I'd like to think I'm resilient, untouchable, but this week has been humbling, to say the least.

As I come in, Beth looks up and chirps, "Good morning, Mr. Aspen."

No matter how early I arrive, she always seems to get here first, already perched efficiently at her desk, hard at work. It's one of the things I admire most about her.

I breathe a sigh of relief at the normalcy of it all. With everything that's been going on, I didn't realize how badly I needed things at the office to feel normal.

"Good morning, Beth," I say, attempting a

smile that I'm sure doesn't reach my eyes. "What's on the agenda today?"

She smiles back, and hers is sincere, if not a little sad. She gazes at her computer, tapping one long fingernail against the screen as she locates the details. "You have a meeting with development at ten, procurement at one thirty, and the board of directors at three. Oh, and Kelly would like to talk to you ASAP."

Of course, the head of PR wants yet another piece of me. All I've done this week so far is help her manage this fucking disaster. It's like wading through a pile of shit—the very definition of unpleasant.

"Tell her I'll call her by lunchtime. There are a few things I want to finish first."

"Can do, sir."

Inhaling deeply, I head into my office and close the door. Then I sit at my desk and stare at my computer like it's the controls to a spaceship. *Fuck* . . . exactly like yesterday. All week, I've been so edgy and off my game, it's been a struggle just to concentrate. My brain feels so scattered, and I can't seem to clear it, no matter what I do.

I rub my eyes and force myself to check my

email, deciding to deal with the non-scandal-related items first. Maybe less excruciating work will help me get a good flow going.

I send the financial analysis team a long list of comments and questions on their latest forecast, only to realize a second too late that I hit REPLY instead of REPLY ALL. *Goddammit.* I resubmit my thoughts and move on to the next email.

For twenty minutes, I attempt to write another few hundred words for the leadership article I've been working on, then change my mind and decide I should talk to our marketing director first. We need to refine our direction for the hotel that's soon to be built in London.

I push my intercom's button. "Beth, can you call Denise and tell her to stop by when she has a moment?"

"I'm . . . afraid not?" She sounds confused.

"What do you mean?"

"She's not in the office this week."

"What? Then where the hell is she?" I snap.

"Attending a B2B conference in Denver. You approved her itinerary several weeks ago."

I detect a hint of reproach in her tone. Or maybe that's just my embarrassment talking.

"Oh . . . right. Sorry, I totally blanked on that." And not only did I forget, I had to make an ass of myself about it too.

"No problem, sir." Her graciousness just makes my gaffe worse. "Would you like me to call her cell instead?"

"No, that's all right. I'll just email her about this, and she'll see it when she gets back."

I hang up, feeling like I'm losing my goddamn mind.

Frustrated, I massage circles into my temples. I absolutely can't let the stress get to me like this. I need about a gallon of coffee—well, what I really need is for those fucking reporters to have kept their mouths shut, but coffee is better than nothing. I almost ask Beth to bring me some, then decide to head downstairs to the cafeteria instead. Maybe getting away from my desk and stretching my legs will help clear my head.

The crowd is at less than half its usual lunchtime peak, and I'm grateful for that, but there are still enough people that the sensation of them staring at me is almost intolerable. I clench my teeth and focus on filling a paper cup with scalding-hot black coffee, and then getting the hell out of there.

Someone walks over to me. Expecting it to be an employee thirsty for details, I reluctantly look up, only to see Oliver.

He gives me a sympathetic smile that I'm really not in the mood for right now. "How you holding up, man?"

I don't need to ask what he's talking about. Everyone who works in this building—maybe everyone in Seattle—has seen that story, and they know it hasn't even come close to dying down.

"Shitty," I reply sourly.

"Yeah, I don't blame you." Oliver scratches his head. "So, uh . . . what're you gonna do about Presley?"

I kind of want to smack him, but that's not fair of me. I knew I'd have to deal with this issue eventually.

I heave a bleak sigh. "I don't see how there's anything I *can* do other than break up with her."

God, I'm the worst kind of idiot. How did I let our relationship get to the point where "breaking up" applies? I'm the one who told her I wasn't looking for anything serious and I wanted to stay casual, and yet here I am, losing my shit over her—in more ways than one.

And now I have to hurt her. I'm sure I've already hurt her.

As I peer down into my cup, I can't help but recall a joke Oliver once made about the way I like my coffee—midnight black—just like my soul, he'd joked. Only now I'm not even sure it was a joke. It sure as fuck doesn't feel like one right now.

Oliver gives me a wry, sympathetic twist of his mouth. "I know it royally sucks. But for what it's worth, I think you're doing the right thing."

Recalling his words in Spokane that day when he warned me away from her, warned me that she was a good girl and I was only going to ruin things, I find they now ring truer than ever. He'd have a viable career in fortune-telling if luxury hotels ever start to bore him.

"I think it's the right thing too." And I really do believe that.

So then why does it feel so wrong? Why is my heart jumping up and down screaming *no*? Why can't I shake the sense that I'm making the biggest mistake of my life? I didn't feel this awful after I had to stop seeing Sara. Presley and I haven't even gotten to the actual breakup yet, and my stomach is already in knots.

Shit . . . our relationship turned way too complicated, way too fast. I promised myself I wouldn't be like this, wouldn't let things go this far. And yet I didn't have the strength to control the situation. One kiss, and I lost all control. One taste, and I threw my rules right out the window.

Oliver pulls me out of my caustic thoughts by squeezing my shoulder. "I'm always here for you, man. Anything you need, just say the word."

"Thanks, Ollie," I say. "Got a time machine lying around?"

He chuckles. "I wish. But I can offer some company for your misery, at least. How about we meet in your office this afternoon and talk about this over whiskey? Maybe we can brainstorm solutions."

I snort despite myself. "Who's *we*? You're the one who drinks at work, not me."

"Come on," he says. "I can pour you just one finger if you're scared. You seriously need to take the edge off before you have an aneurysm."

I roll my eyes. "As long as you stop pestering me about it, you have yourself a deal. I'll have a little and see if it helps. At this point, I'll try anything."

"Attaboy." He looks almost smug.

"I'm free after four."

Oliver nods. "Perfect. I'll swing by then."

As we walk back to the office, my phone buzzes. It's a text from Presley.

We need to talk.

My stomach tightens. This is it. I didn't think the moment of truth would come quite so soon, but I have to face it regardless. I have to stay strong and do what's best for both of us. Even if it eats me up inside.

Taking a deep breath, I type back:

Agreed. You pick the place.

She replies with an address I've never been to, along with the time of nine p.m. tonight.

I nod. Neutral territory. Outside of work hours.

Makes sense.

Now I just have to figure out what in the hell I'm going to say to her.

• • •

At Oliver's insistence, my girls and I are having dinner at his and Jess's apartment tonight. He thought I could use a night off from my apparent *self-loathing*. His words, not mine.

Jess greets us at the door with a warm hug for each of my daughters and a bright smile for me. Maybe it's too much to hope for, but I'm not sure she's heard the news yet. I find it doubtful that Oliver didn't tell her—they're as thick as thieves, these two, and have been since college.

"Sorry about all your troubles, handsome," Jess says, still smiling at me, but with a look of sympathy in her eyes. "It'll pass, you know?"

I guess I have my answer. I nod, grumbling, "I know."

She smiles sadly and pats my hand.

With that, we make our way into the kitchen where homemade macaroni and cheese is being prepared, along with a big pot of spicy chili and cornbread.

"It smells great, Jess. Can I help?" I ask, surveying the countertops. There's no sign of Oliver, but he left right after we shared a drink in my office, so I'm assuming he's here somewhere.

She gives her head a shake. "I've got everything under control. Figured you guys could use some comfort food."

"Thoughtful of you, thank you."

She nods, then gazes down at the girls. "Uncle Ollie is in the den, setting up for a tea party I hear never got finished from the last time he was over."

"Tea party!" Lacey and Emilia both squeal at once and scramble from the kitchen toward the adjoining den.

I watch them go, their feet clapping across the hardwood floors as quickly as their chubby legs will carry them.

When I hear Oliver's voice from the other room, and then laughter, I smile for the first time all day and release a slow exhale.

Then Oliver strolls into the kitchen and gives my hand a shake. "I'm glad you came."

I nod. He knows me well. I almost didn't. Hiding out at home in the dark where I could sulk properly sounded pretty damn appealing. But then I'd just end up watching the news on repeat and feeling even more miserable and helpless than I do already.

"Everything's just about done. Oliver, pour some drinks, would ya, babe?" Jess says, giving the chili one final stir.

After peeking in the other room to check on the girls, I lean one hip against the counter and watch as the final dinner preparations are made.

Seeing Oliver and Jess together, it's . . . I don't know . . . nice. Domestic. Blissful.

It surprises me how much I enjoy watching them as they move comfortably together in the kitchen—him helping her reach a high cabinet, her finishing his sentences. The tender looks they give each other. My thoughts flash to Presley, and something kicks hard inside my chest.

This could be us, a voice whispers inside my head.

Yes, but that would mean giving up my entire way of life.

But it wouldn't feel like "giving up" when you'd be gaining so much.

Christ. I shake my head. Now I'm answering the voices inside my head? Even I know that's not a good sign.

"Are you all right, Dom?" Oliver asks, giving me a strange look.

I swallow. "Just hungry," I lie. "Everything smells terrific."

Jess smiles kindly at me, pausing with oven mitts on both hands to look at me. "Maybe you need a good woman in your life. Someone who can cook for you and take care of you. You deserve it, you know? And one stupid news story doesn't change that."

Oliver chuckles darkly. "Oh no, didn't you know? Dom here is going to die old and lonely. It's his lot in life."

Jess scoffs, throwing me a pointed look over her shoulder on the way to the oven. "I said what I said."

As we sit down to dinner, I still haven't been able to quiet the voices inside my head, but two things are certain: there's a strange pinching feeling inside my chest, and I'm more eager than ever to talk with Presley in a few hours.

CHAPTER TWENTY-ONE
Presley

The sun just set, and with it, all the warmth was sucked from the city, it seems. Today was cooler than usual for July, and the evening air is damp.

Tugging my sweater tighter around me, I check the maps app on my phone to make sure I'm walking in the right direction. If the GPS is accurate, then Moon and Stars Lounge and Bar should be right here. I frown, looking at the barbershop where the tarot card parlor should be.

Turning, I finally spot it—an unassuming narrow staircase that leads down toward a dark wooden door with a silver crescent moon nailed to it.

A little chill of excitement runs down my spine. I was surprised when Dominic agreed to meet me here. It was a place neither of us had been, which would ensure it would be neutral ground.

He said that I could name the place, so why not pick a spot I've been dreaming of coming to for months?

I walk into the dimly lit lounge and wait for my eyes to adjust to the dark. The door swings closed behind me. The lounge is all velvet and low-hanging lights, with a bar at the far back of the room. Art on the walls depicts the goddesses in all their beauty and ferocious glory. It's surprisingly fuller than I thought it would be.

When I can make out the shadowy figures, huddled over their tables with glasses of wine, I find the silhouette I'm looking for. As I gaze at the line of his broad shoulders and the curl of hair at the nape of his neck . . . a little pang of worry shivers through me, and I desperately want to turn and run back to Bianca's apartment and bury myself in her couch cushions.

This is going to be impossible.

"Hey," I say, keeping my composure.

Dominic turns, his eyes so dark and empty that I almost take a step back in shock.

I take in everything in a matter of seconds.

Thick eyelashes. A strong jaw. Too pretty of a

mouth. The notch of an Adam's apple peeking out above his shirt collar. He's perfection, but he looks more somber than I've ever seen him—even if he's trying hard to hide it.

"Presley." Dominic stands from the table and pulls out a chair for me.

I take a seat, acutely aware of how stiff we're both acting. A glass of water is waiting for me, so I take a greedy gulp.

"This is quite the little spot," he says, his gaze flitting from table to table. "I ordered a drink, and they asked me what my zodiac sign is."

"What is your sign?" I ask, intrigued.

"Aquarius," he says, then gives me a curious look. "What?"

"No, it's just . . . of course you're an Aquarius." I should have known from the beginning. The rebellious nature, the desire for innovation, the need for emotional freedom . . . it all makes sense.

"I'm not a big water person. I don't love swimming."

"Aquarius is an air sign," I say with a smirk into my glass of water.

"Ah, well, you're the smart one. So, what are you?"

"Hmm?"

"What's your sign?"

"Scorpio."

He shudders dramatically. "That sounds intimidating."

"We're conniving . . . vindictive." I smile sweetly. "But also loyal friends and lovers. Ride or die, as they say."

"Ride or die," he repeats, as if he's never heard the phrase before.

He raises his glass of whiskey to my water, and we clink them together amiably. Sitting here, talking like we're on our first date . . . it's definitely weird.

Better to cut to the chase.

"Anyway. There's something I want—"

"Do you want a real drink? Let me get you a drink." Suddenly, he's on his feet and heading toward the bar.

Okay . . .

He has to know why I asked him here. He knows we need to talk. Is he avoiding it?

When he returns with a tall glass of bubbly, I smile. *At least he knows my drink.*

"Thank you," I say. I clear my throat, attempting to summon the courage I need in order to have this conversation. I practiced it in the mirror this morning, ran it by Bianca before I left, and even rehearsed it on the walk here.

How hard is it to tell an emotionally unavailable man you're in love with him?

A woman wearing a long purple gown makes her way to our table. In her hands is a stack of beautifully illustrated tarot cards. The drawings are intricate, moons and flowers and hands and hearts—all the makings for a beautiful deck. The gilded edges catch in the candlelight like jewelry.

"A reading?" she asks, presenting the cards before us.

"No, thanks," I say. I need to get these words out before I explode, lady. Can't you see we're in the middle of something?

"Can she use your cards?" Dominic asks suddenly. He turns to me, meeting my surprised gaze.

"What? You read, don't you?"

The woman turns to me with an amused tilt of the head.

Oh my God. This is so humiliating.

"I—sometimes. My grandmother taught me," I stammer, feeling my cheeks growing rosier by the second. Tarot cards have been a very private part of my life, and to suddenly be facing a professional—well, it's humbling. I really don't want some stranger listening in.

But without another word, the woman places the stack of cards in the center of our table and gives me a reassuring wink. Then she walks away, her long skirts brushing the floor behind her.

"They're bigger than I thought they would be," Dominic says, brushing his fingers against the deck.

It's so hard to be sitting here with him, with all of his masculine beauty and strength and his quiet confidence, and with the heartbreaking knowledge that he's not mine. Knowing I can't touch him. Knowing he left a huge hole in my heart.

I release a short sigh. So far this isn't going how I planned.

"Do you actually want me to read your cards?" I ask, a little unsure of his intentions.

Do I want to read his cards? I admit I'm fiendishly curious.

"Sure." His tone is casual, even if he doesn't appear entirely relaxed.

I contemplate the decision for a moment. Maybe the cards will help me say what I want to say to him. They've never failed me before. And maybe it's crazy, but using the cards helps me feel closer to my grandma, and my mom too. I could use a little motherly wisdom right about now.

"Okay." I shuffle the deck, piece by piece, the way I was taught. "The way I do tarot is just for beginners. It is only as accurate as you let it be."

"I have an open mind," he says.

"All right. Cut the deck into three stacks," I tell him, and he does. "Now, reveal the leftmost card. This card will give us insight into your past."

"The Emperor?" he says, scrutinizing the bearded man in the picture. "What does it mean?"

"The Emperor is the father figure, which is very appropriate for you. In your recent past, you became a father to two little girls, and also inherited an enterprise from your own father. You have become a father in both your personal and professional lives, in a sense. But it's not just the Emperor. It's the Reversed Emperor. See how it's facing me instead of you?"

"What does that mean?" His brows push together.

I wonder briefly if showing my new boss / ex-lover his spiritual flaws is really the best way to ensure a happy working relationship.

Fuck it.

"It means you are—or were—exercising too much control on your own life. Your inflexibility was stifling the natural flow of events."

Dominic furrows his brow, making me wonder if I've already lost him. "Continue."

"Turn over the next card. This will give us insight into your present."

We both lean in to see what the cards will reveal.

The Hangman. *Interesting.* I rarely get this card. I have to dig into my banks of knowledge for this one.

"That seems ominous," he mutters into his whiskey before taking a slow drink.

"Not at all. The Hangman is actually representative of letting go. And since it's upright, it means that you are excelling in it. You're moving in the right direction. That's good!"

Without thinking, I reach out and grasp Dom's hand in a gesture meant to comfort, but the moment my skin touches his, a shock reverberates through both of us. I can tell by the way his lips part that he feels it too. I pull my hand back, chastising myself for crossing that physical boundary.

Dominic clears his throat. "Let me guess," he says, pointing at the last unturned card. "The future?"

"Yes," I say. My stomach churns.

He flips the card just enough for his own eyes to see. Then he lets it slide from his fingers, still facedown.

"What is it?" I ask, curious to see what he's hiding.

He gazes straight into my eyes. "I can't be with you, Presley."

This time, his rejection is like getting punched

in the throat. I feel the lump form like a bruise and lodge itself in my trachea. I can't speak. Can't breathe.

"I'm sorry," he says, his voice cutting through me like a cold wind.

"No," I manage to croak. "I'm sorry."

"You have nothing to be sorry for." He shakes his head, roughly rubbing his eyes with the heal of his hand.

"I do, though," I say, my voice wobbling. "You told me not to fall in love with you. I did it anyway. I guess I'm not very good at following directions."

Tears now falling freely from my eyes roll down both cheeks, and I quickly wipe them away. But I'm not ashamed. It feels so good to just say it out loud. I hadn't imagined that I would ever get this far. I thought he would retreat before I got the chance to bare my soul like this. But I'm not hiding my truth any longer.

"I don't have the capacity for love," he says softly, his eyes downcast at the table in front of us.

"That's stupid."

He looks up at me in shock.

"I mean, for a CEO, you're really dumb. You *are* capable of love. I've seen it in the way you take care of your daughters. And in the way that you look to Fran for help and advice when you need it most. I've seen it in the way that you work with Oliver. You trust him, more than anyone. I've seen it when you talk about your brother that you lost. I've seen it when you first gave me that promotion—"

Dominic opens his mouth to object.

"—and don't pretend that was strictly professional. You care about me and my future. I saw it when I was with Emilia and Lacey, braiding their hair. I know you felt it."

"Presley . . ."

"That *is* love. Love is messy and imperfect. It isn't that you aren't capable of it. It's that you're overwhelmed by it."

Dominic is stunned silent. I can't quite make out the meaning behind the look in his eyes. I've way overstepped what is appropriate to say to one's boss, but any and all boundaries crumbled into dust the first time he kissed me.

"I can't keep working for you," I blurt out. "If you can't be with me in the way that we both need you to be, then I'm going to walk away. It's the only way."

These aren't the words I planned on saying, but as soon as they're out of my mouth, I'm flooded with a sense of relief, knowing they're the right ones. There's no way I can work alongside him now—this man who took my virginity, took my whole heart, and offered me nothing in return. If I'm going to pick up the pieces, I need to do it where I won't be constantly hiding from his shadow.

The silence is deafening, and other people in the lounge are shooting curious glances our way. I've made a scene. This isn't how I wanted to say it. I wanted to be strong, aloof even.

I pull a tissue from my purse, wipe away the tears, and quietly blow my nose. I won't look at him. I must seem like an immature lovesick idiot to him, and I couldn't bear to see myself through his eyes right now.

When I look up, he's placed his final card directly in front of me. I pick it up with shaking fingers. *The Lovers.*

His voice is soft as he says, "I might be totally awful at this relationship thing."

Still unable to meet his eyes, I feel the air shift

between us. *What's happening?*

Dominic takes a deep breath. "I might be insensitive. I might not know when you're hurting, or when you need me. I might need a lot of space."

The words fall out of his mouth like salts into a warm bath, easing the knot in my stomach and the lump in my throat.

As if he can read my mind, he lifts my chin with his finger. My lower lip quivers, and his gaze falls to my mouth. With one movement, he leans across the table and kisses me tenderly on the lips. My hands find his under the table. When he releases me, he drops his forehead against mine, our hands tangled together, an array of forgotten cards scattered in front of us.

"I can't lose you," he murmurs. "I need you, Presley."

"What does that mean? I can't keep doing this. This back-and-forth with you."

"I know you can't. And the truth is, neither can I."

"What are you saying?"

He pauses, his stormy eyes on mine. "I've felt for so long that I was unlovable. That I had too much baggage, and that no one would possibly want to take that on. To be with me—to accept me and all of my many flaws."

I smile at him sadly. "That's not even a little bit true, Dom." I can't help but think of his ex that discarded him and their babies like they meant absolutely nothing to her.

He takes a deep breath, releasing it slowly. "I don't deserve you."

"I go after what I want." I shrug, trying to lighten the mood.

"I can see that." He smiles. "I want you too, Presley. I shouldn't. But I'm selfish and I do. There's no one else."

I feel like I could float away. My eyes flutter closed. The anxiety in my chest unknots, and I let out a breathless laugh.

"What do you—" I start to ask before he cuts me off with a hard kiss. I pull him close to me, leaning far across the table for a better angle. With every push of my lips against his, I want him to feel exactly how much he means to me. And by the way he kisses me back, I really think he does.

Pulling back a few inches, Dominic touches

my cheek, meeting my eyes with a soft expression. "How can you just forgive me so easily? I paid you after we had sex, for fuck's sake. And in London I was so cold. I acted like a complete and total prick."

I swallow down a sudden lump of emotion. He's not known for dramatic emotional displays or baring his soul like this. It's a big moment for him, and his apology means everything to me. He was cold in London, that's true, but he was still hurting then. I see that now. It was a defense mechanism.

"You're not a prick, Dominic. You're human. We mess up sometimes." My voice is soft and I meet his eyes, amazed at all the emotion I see reflected back at me.

"That's putting it mildly," he murmurs.

I shake my head. "Don't you think I have regrets? That whole thing with Austin—signing up for Allure?" I'd done plenty of stupid things to jeopardize our future too.

His hand slides from my cheek to cup the back of my neck, his warm fingers sinking into my hair. "Let's start over then. We can't run from our mistakes, but we can put them behind us."

"That's the smartest thing you've said all

week." I grin at him, the knot of worry in my chest totally gone now.

"How are you so confident about all of this relationship shit?" He chuckles when we part for a shaky breath. "I have no idea what I'm doing."

"Oh God, neither do I," I admit. "Does this make me a stepmom? I'm not sure if I would be a good stepmom, or even a mom, for that matter. I want to be, but I—"

"You're just Presley. That's all they want." He uses his thumb to wipe a stray tear from my cheek. "That's all I want."

"I may be bad at it," I whisper. Part of me knows I should be terrified, but the thing is, it's so easy when I'm with them.

He leans in to kiss me again. It's slow and sweet and affectionate. Then he whispers against my lips, "I find it very hard to believe that there's anything you're not good at."

CHAPTER TWENTY-TWO

Dominic

Four months later

Presley, Francine, and I are in the kitchen, taking turns cooking and diverting the twins away from the myriad hot and pointy objects in play, when the doorbell rings.

"Go ahead. I've got things under control here," Francine says.

I glance up from tending my potful of bubbling potatoes. "You sure?"

"Of course—you're the hosts. Now shoo, dearies." She flicks her hand at us with a smile.

We answer the door to a young man I recognize from photos as Presley's brother, and an affable-looking guy with brown eyes and a mop of unruly black curls.

"Thank you for coming. I'm Dominic."

Michael shakes my hand, and when he smiles, I can see the resemblance between him and Presley right away. They share the same curious blue eyes and high cheekbones. "Thanks for the invite. This is Elijah."

"Make yourselves at home," I say, stepping aside to let them in.

Presley hugs Michael and pecks him on the cheek. "I'm so glad you could make it."

"I wouldn't miss Thanksgiving with my big sister," he replies with a grin.

"And Elijah," she says, smiling. "It's so nice to meet you. I've heard good things."

"Then they're all true," Elijah says.

Michael shoots a grin at the other boy that's so adoring, I almost expect cartoon hearts to float up around their heads.

Ah, young love . . . wait, did I really just think that? Dammit, being a dad has made me prematurely old.

Her eyes sparkling, Presley leans toward Michael. "Are you two exclusive yet?"

"Sis . . ." Michael groans, like the teenager he so recently was.

"We're glad you're here," I say. Everyone smiles and the awkwardness dissolves, which is what I was hoping for. I shake Elijah's hand too. "Thanks for coming."

"Thank you for having me, Mr. Aspen," he replies.

Points for politeness. "Please, call me Dominic. Dinner should be ready in twenty minutes—"

"Half an hour," Francine yells from the kitchen. "It's a big old bird."

"What she said. But you can have some appetizers while you wait."

Francine makes a noise of surprise, and I'm hoping she didn't just chop off her finger or something.

"Presley, can you show them to the dining room while I go get that?"

"You have a whole dining room in your apartment?" Michael asks, wide-eyed.

"I know, right? This place is huge," Presley says as she leads them off.

After checking on Francine (it was merely an excited squeal because her gravy is *perfect*), I bring in a plate of appetizers to set on the table. Lacey and Emilia follow me, but at the sight of strangers, they hide behind my legs, too shy to come forward, yet too curious to scurry back to Francine.

"Meet my daughters, Emilia and Lacey." I point to each twin as I say her name.

Michael and Elijah squat down to greet the girls with friendly smiles.

"Hi, guys," Michael says. "Nice to meet you. I'm Presley's brother, Michael, and this is my boyfriend, Elijah."

"You're a boy," Lacey says, poking her head out.

Grinning, Elijah nods. "I sure am."

"Why?" Emilia asks.

"That's a fantastically complicated question." Elijah chuckles. "Guess I should've brought my Gender Studies textbook."

Michael explains. "Sometimes love just works like that. Anybody can love anybody."

The girls think about that for a moment, then

nod, apparently satisfied.

"If only it were that easy with Dad," Presley jokes.

Michael rolls his eyes with a derisive laugh. "No kidding."

I hum noncommittally. "Let's go take over for Francine. She'll insist she doesn't need any help, but she deserves a break."

Presley and I head back into the kitchen to resume mashing potatoes, simmering cranberry relish, and prepping the pumpkin pie for baking. Through the doorway leading into the dining room, we can catch glimpses of my girls entertaining our guests, and hear snippets of conversation and laughter.

"This is nice," Presley murmurs. "Having the apartment full and busy, I mean. I wouldn't want to do it every day, but it's so . . . cozy."

I drop a kiss on her forehead. "Yeah, it really feels like a home."

When there's another knock on the door, I scramble to wash my hands.

"I'll get it," I say, my heart beating a little faster. I'm pretty confident I've planned this well, but now that the moment is actually here, it's nerve-racking, mostly because I have no idea if I'm doing the right thing.

I open the door. "George?" I've never seen him in person before. I can tell where Presley gets her nose from.

The thin, gray-haired man on my threshold nods. "And you must be Dominic. Very nice place you got here."

When I lead him into the dining room, Presley stops in midsentence and goes as rigid as a statue. Michael takes a step back, and Elijah grabs his hand. At everyone else's reactions, Francine stands up protectively, and the girls zip to her side, wary.

"How did you know where we were?" Presley says in the coldest tone I've ever heard from her.

George offers an uncertain, placating half smile. "Dominic invited me."

She whips around to stare at me. "Wait, you did *what*?"

Shit, she can be intimidating when she wants to be. It's almost enough to make me flinch—and also a tiny bit hot, but let's not go there right now.

"He has an apology for you," I say.

Her shock and anger rapidly drain away to bewilderment. She looks back at her father. "You . . . do?"

Solemn, he nods, sucking his teeth. "Dominic called me a week or two ago. He helped me see that I have two kids I'm immensely proud of. I'm sorry I lost sight of that with your mom gone. I lost my way and I fu—" He glances down at the girls, clinging to Francine's legs. "I did nothing but let my children down. I promise I'll try harder and do better from now on."

Presley's expression softens a little. "Mom's death was hard on all of us. And while you did hurt us both, we still love you." She chews her lip. "But if you can't accept Michael for who he is, then this isn't going to work. That's a deal breaker for us both."

Hesitant, George looks over at Michael and Elijah, who are keeping their faces neutral but are gripping each other's hands so tightly their knuckles are white. Presley watches the three of them with wary eyes, like she's ready to throw herself in front of a bullet if need be.

Finally, George extends his hand to Elijah. "As long as you treat my son well, we're good."

Everyone smiles in relief, and Michael releases a huge breath, tears threatening to fall. Elijah shakes George's offered hand with the one that's not still clutching Michael's.

The girls creep forward shyly, and Lacey tugs on George's pant leg.

"You're Grandpa?"

Presley and I gawk at Lacey, then each other, then George, who's equally confused. The other three adults stifle a laugh.

Her lips twitching, Francine says, "Now, sweetheart . . ."

"I can sure try." George looks back to us. "Only if you two are okay with that, of course."

"Uhhh," we both say.

"They're your kids, so it's your call," Presley tells me.

Drop the whole decision on me, why don't ya. She's practically their stepmom already, but I don't want to get into that discussion in front of everyone.

I rub my chin, musing. "I guess we can do a trial run."

George turns back to the girls with a smile. "Looks like the answer is yes."

"I'm hungry," Emilia reminds us.

I scoop her up onto my hip. "An excellent point, darling. Let's eat!"

• • •

Late into the night, my home remained so full of joy, light, and warmth, eating and drinking and laughter. Now the guests have gone, the halls are dark, my girls sleeping peacefully down the hall. Presley and I are curled up together in my bed . . . and this feels like family too.

"Are we going to talk about your surprise today? What made you think of it?" Presley asks, her head pillowed on my chest.

I run my fingers through her elegant spill of dark hair. Her relationship with her father is something that has been on my mind for a long time, actually. Maybe it's because I'm a dad now as well and could never imagine not having a relationship with my daughters. But it was more than that too.

"Well, I never got a chance to reconcile with my father . . . or protect my brother . . . but I figured

I could still help you with yours."

She props herself on her elbow to stroke my stubbled cheek, sympathy in her eyes. "I'm sorry, Dominic."

I still don't know how to handle it when she looks at me like that, when I can see the full, over-whelming depth of what she feels for me. "You don't have to be sorry. It's in the past."

"The past can still hurt," she says softly.

"It can. But I have a present to take care of . . . and a future to look forward to."

We lie together for a while, just enjoying each other's warm solidarity. Then, in a much lighter tone, she asks, "So, what on earth did you say to convince my dad?"

"A magician never reveals his secrets," I say, not because I actually don't want to tell her, but because I want to make her laugh.

She does and nudges me in the ribs playfully. "Oh, come on, I'm dying to know. Dad almost nev-er apologizes."

"Well, I said a lot of things—some of which I can't repeat in front of the girls—but I think what did the trick was finding some common ground. I told him I'm a single father too, and I understand how hard it can be when your children's mother isn't there, and how easy it is for your life to get out of hand. But if he lets these family relationships go, he'll regret it until the day he dies."

Blinking fast, she sniffles wetly.

"Are you oka—"

Her fervent kiss cuts me off. "I love you so much," she says hoarsely, squeezing me tight.

My heart soars to the heavens, as it always does every time I hear those words. "I love you too," I murmur against her lips.

To think, barely any time ago I never would have let myself think that, let alone say it out loud. But now I can. Every hour of every day until forever ends.

She kisses me again, hungry and joyful, and I answer with everything I have. Our touches quickly turn from sweet to hot, and soon I'm helping Presley push her pajama bottoms off.

"Can't wake the kids," she says, already breathless under me.

"I can keep quiet if you can." I nip at her neck.

She makes a torn, needy noise. "I'll try."

Sliding into her is yet another kind of coming home. We rock together, slow and sensual, as if we have all the time in the world—because now we do. I marvel at that knowledge, luxuriate in it, in her body and her moans and the love shining from her eyes.

"Y-you're not making this easy," she pants.

"Sorry. I just can't help myself when it comes to you." I kiss her, sealing in our sounds of pleasure, and repeat the move until she's clutching at my back and whimpering into my mouth.

I thrust faster, harder, and she bucks up to meet me. My hands run over her hungrily, caressing every inch of skin I can reach. My whole body is tensing, nerves sparking, so intense, and it's clear she's quickly getting closer too. Her muffled moans come louder and more urgent, washing heat over me. With every second, I fall deeper into Presley until nothing else exists.

Suddenly, her trembling turns into full-body quakes. At the sensation of her arching and writhing beneath me, clenching in waves around my cock, I can't hold out any longer. Pleasure sweeps over me like a tsunami—with a long, rough-edged groan, I follow her over the edge. When our bliss ebbs away, I wrap her in my arms.

As we lay entwined, sated and tired and content, our eyes meet, and I can see the promise of a vast new future spread out before us. Whatever comes next, I will never be the same again. *And I'm so ready.*

I nuzzle into her neck. "Hey . . . can I ask you something?"

"Yeah?" she mumbles sleepily.

"Do you want to, um, move in with me?"

She sits up and stares at me, blinking. Then a smile spreads across her face that's so beautiful, it almost stops my heart.

"Are you serious?"

"Completely," I say, returning her smile. "I want you here with me. With the girls."

She chews on her lip, considering this. "But do you think it will be okay, I mean . . ."

I quiet her by taking her hand and guiding her lips to mine. "They love you, Presley, almost as much as I do. It's going to be perfect."

Her eyes find mine, and she looks so happy that

it makes my heart clench. "Then I'd love to."

EPILOGUE

Dominic

Three years later

The girls said we could drop them off at the school's curb and Presley thirded the motion, saying the building wasn't that big. But I vetoed that idea. No way am I going to abandon them to fumble their own way to their classroom. Maybe in a few weeks . . . or years . . . but definitely not today.

It's their very first day of kindergarten, after all. The first time they've been away from home *all day long* without me, Presley, or Francine.

As we escort them through the halls, I'm fidgeting like crazy, twisting my wedding ring around and around my finger. "You sure you've got your lunches in your backpacks? You know what to do if you need to come home?"

"Call Franny," Emilia answers dutifully. Lacey is already distracted, taking in the colorful posters and noisy crowd all around us with a wide-eyed grin.

"And do you remember her number?"

"Um . . ."

"Dom," Presley says. "Relax. The teacher has Francine's number. And our numbers, and their pediatrician's, and the National Guard's . . ."

I frown. "I know that. It's just an extra precaution."

"And this is just a school—a private school, even," she says. "It's only until three. Francine will pick them up and take them home, and we'll see them again tonight."

"You say 'only three,' but that's six hours away. What if they miss us during the day? What if they need help using the potty? What if the other kids are mean? What if they don't eat their lunch? You know they've been so picky lately. What if—"

Presley squeezes my shoulder, loving but firm. "Honey. *Chill out.* Stop acting like we're throwing them to the wolves."

"Wolves? Can I see?" Emilia asks.

"It's only a figure of speech, honey. The only wolves around here are at the zoo."

"I'm perfectly chill," I say, frowning. "But we have to be sure they're ready."

"Somehow I don't think they're the ones who aren't ready," Presley teases. "Seriously, they can handle it. They're more than old enough, and they did great in preschool."

"But preschool was only a half day. This might—"

"I'm a big girl," Lacey says.

"Yes, you are, sweet pea. I quite agree." Presley squats down. "Show me on your hands?"

After thinking for a few moments, Lacey holds up five fingers.

"And how many is that?"

Lacey says, "Five," at the same instant Emilia answers for her. "Five!"

Presley shoots a smile back over her shoulder at me before asking them, "And how much do Mommy and Daddy and Franny love you?"

"Infinity!" they both shout, flinging their arms open wide.

"Absolutely right." She hugs them, then stands up again. "See? They're rocket scientists." She lays her hand gently on my arm. "We always knew we'd have to let go sometime."

Throwing her arms around my hips, Emilia says, "Don't cry, Daddy."

"Yeah, we're gonna be okay!" Lacey says, trying to reassure me.

I have to laugh at how thoroughly we've switched roles here. "Thanks, you two. But for your information, I'm not crying. A bug just flew into my eye." I wipe my sleeve across my face.

Shit. I am totally about to cry. *What's happening to me?*

"Are you ready, girls?" their teacher calls.

After one last round of kisses, they run inside and the door shuts behind them. If I squint through the frosted glass, I can just barely see the blobs of color that belong to our precious daughters. Then they move farther into the classroom and are lost.

Presley pats my lower back. "Poor thing. You're going to be useless at the office today, aren't you?"

"Oh, hush," I grunt.

"But, seriously, I love this side to you. It's adorable." Taking my hand, she kisses me warmly.

I level her with a heated look. "Did you just call me adorable?"

She chuckles, lacing her fingers through mine. "Yes. But don't worry, I'll cheer you up later."

Smirking, I raise her hand to my lips to kiss the back of it, right over her exquisite diamond ring. It feels like I gave it to her a whole lifetime ago, and it feels like no time at all. "Promise?"

She beams at me. "Always and forever."

• • •

My wife was right about one thing—I'm completely useless at the office. Thankfully, my calendar is mostly clear. I suspect that she and Beth had something to do with that fact, like they knew kindergarten drop-off would hit me hard. Hell, I didn't even know it would, but I'm thankful there are more than a few smart women in my life.

Presley has a busy day today, and so I barely see her after we arrive. She's no longer the director of operations, she now runs the entire international operation, and she has, flawlessly, for two years now.

From my desk, I check her calendar and see that she has a lunch with her friend Bianca in a little while. Bianca got married last spring and is pregnant with her first baby—a little girl. Presley has been saving our girls' hand-me-down clothes ever since the gender-reveal party.

My gaze slips past the meetings until I find what I'm looking for. We have a six o'clock dinner with Presley's dad, Grandpa George, along with her brother, Michael, and his fiancé, Elijah.

My days before Presley came crashing into it were filled with work and parental obligations. But since I finally got my head out of my ass and accepted that she was part of my future—and that I did deserve to be loved—now my days are filled with family and laughter and so much love, I hardly recognize it.

"Knock-knock," a familiar voice calls from the door.

"Hey. Come on in," I say, glancing up to spot Oliver lingering at the threshold.

He's a little more gun-shy about barging straight into my office without knocking, ever since that time last year he caught me bending Presley over my desk. In our defense, it was after hours, and we assumed everyone was gone for the day. Thankfully, he didn't catch a glimpse of anything more than my bare ass. Though I guess that was enough to traumatize him.

"Is it safe?" he jokes.

I roll my eyes. "'Course it is. What's up?"

Oliver drops into the chair in front of my desk and shrugs. "Presley set up an eleven o'clock meeting on my calendar saying that I was supposed to come check on you because today was the first day of school drop-off or something?"

I stifle a sigh. *She has my entire staff in on this?* I would complain, but sadly, they like her more than they like me. And Oliver's totally a lost cause—he's wrapped around her finger. Both he and Jess adore her.

"I'm fine. Now go get back to work."

Oliver stands to his feet, shaking his head. "Jeez. Touchy today."

I grin at his retreating frame. "Thanks, Ollie."

I've barely gotten through my next email when there's someone else at my door. I hear the click of heels and look up. It's my lovely wife.

A smile lifts my lips as I watch her walk toward me. Bypassing the desk, she comes around behind it and slips into my lap.

I grin in surprise when she seats herself on top of me. "Hi there."

"Hi." She presses a quick kiss to my lips.

She's not normally so touchy-feely at the office, and I can't help but wonder if she's checking on me too. I'll be honest, I don't hate it.

"I'm okay, you know?" I raise one eyebrow at her.

She laughs. "I know you are. I just wanted to see if you needed anything before I head out to meet Bianca."

Tightening my arms around her, I hold her close, and Presley sighs. "Just you."

She smiles, bringing her lips to mine again. "You have me."

"Go have fun at lunch. I'll just be here sulking, watching the clock." I sigh for dramatic effect, and she swats my chest.

"You're a big baby. I told you I'll make it up to you later." She stands and adjusts my tie before she starts toward the door.

"Best intern I ever hired," I call to her retreating backside, and I hear Presley chuckle.

It's the absolute truth. Although, to be fair, Presley was never *just* an intern. She was the woman who rocked my entire world from the first time I laid eyes on her. And now she's mine.

Forever and always.

• • •

If you enjoyed Seven Nights of Sin, you are going to love my next release, ***Playing for Keeps***.

Turn the page for a preview of this cocky foulmouthed hockey player and the sassy heroine who knocks him off his game.

HOT JOCKS 1

PLAYING
FOR KEEPS

My entire body feels like I've been in a car accident—from my pounding head to the unexplainably sore muscles below my waist.

My mouth is bone dry, and as I blink open my eyes, I have to focus on my breathing to calm the queasiness in my stomach.

Whose bed did I fall asleep in?

I shift to my side and it takes me several long seconds to realize where the hell I am.

Panic hits me the moment my eyes focus.

I look over my shoulder and see that a very naked Justin Brady is still asleep beside me.

His broad back with its lightly tanned skin slopes down to the most mouth-watering naked ass I've ever seen on a man. Firm. Muscled. Delectable.

A thousand vivid mental images crash into my brain at once. My hands on that firm, rounded ass as he thrust into me. Those trim hips snapping between my parted thighs.

I whimper, and scramble over the side of the bed in a hunt for my clothes. And my sanity, because what the hell did I do last night? What did *we* do last night?

I remember coming in here to use the bathroom. Remember finding Justin sitting on his bed, looking somber. Then I remember kissing him. Oh my God, the kissing. I feel weak at the memory of his hot, wet tongue sliding against mine.

I find my underwear first, and pull those on— inside out, but who cares about that right now. I toss on my bra and jersey next. The jersey with my brother's number on the back. *Oh my God, Owen.* He's going to kill me if he sees me leaving Justin's room. Actually, he'll kill Justin first. And it will be bloody. I can't witness Justin's murder this morning. Because I will definitely vomit on the floor if that happens.

My leggings are nowhere to be found. I can't exactly sneak out of here pantless. *Fuck me. What had I been thinking?* I'd always lusted after Justin, but secretly lusting after him and sleeping with him are two very, *very* different things.

Yet I distinctly remember being the one to push

things further. We'd been kissing on his bed, and I'd been the one to take off my shirt and then his hands traveled along my waist, my ribs, my shoulders. His touch had been my undoing —I'd been the first one to stick my hand down his pants. It was like throwing accelerant onto the fire quietly burning between us.

How drunk had he been? Way drunker than me, I know that much. Had I taken advantage of him?

Just as I'm about to have a full-blown panic attack, I spot my leggings. They're tangled in the sheets at the end of the bed. The memory of Justin kneeling before me as he slowly peeled them off jumps into my head. I'd been so hot, so ready for him. I remember practically attacking his belt-buckle with gusto in my efforts to free his erection.

Oh my God. His dick.

Now that I've pictured it, I can't unsee it. The memory of his steely shaft and heavy balls are not details I'm supposed to be in possession of. The helpless plea he'd made when my fist curled around him for the first time, testing the weight of him against my palm… I'd dragged my hand up slowly as he released a shuddering exhale, his whole body shivering.

My heartrate triples with the memory. I squeeze my eyes shut and pull a deep, shaky breath into my lungs. *Focus, Elise.* You cannot think about his dick right now. You certainly can't think about the way it tasted, or how it felt …

Tiptoeing to the end of the bed, I reach for my leggings, and give them a swift tug. Justin shifts at the movement, rolling up on his elbow to see who's woken him. His dark hair is messy from sleep, but his blue eyes are bright and alert. A five o'clock shadow dusts his strong jaw and his chest muscles are immaculate.

I don't think I've ever used the word immaculate to describe someone before, but trust me, it fits him.

His eyes widen as he takes in the sight of me—standing at the end of his bed, naked from the waist down—and he blinks twice. "Elise?" his voice is pure gravel, and my stomach tightens.

"Yeah?"

Realizing he's naked, Justin sits up, tugging the sheet up to cover his lap, like he's suddenly self-conscious—like he wasn't inside me a few hours ago.

Oh God.

He's still watching me but he doesn't say anything else as I free my leggings from the blankets and pull them on. Yeah, I really might vomit. *Shit, this is awful.*

He pushes one hand through his messy hair, his bicep flexing with the effort. "Last night …" Confusion is etched across his gorgeous features as he works on remembering what happened, and I swear to God, if he doesn't say something in the next three seconds, I'm going to cry.

Tears threaten behind my eyes and I take another slow, shaky breath.

Some part of me needs him to acknowledge this mountain between us. Needs him to laugh and make some joke that we've really *cemented our friendship now*— or any lighthearted remark that will make last night mean something more than just being a colossal mistake, a huge dark mark on our friendship. I need him to say something that will make it all better. *Anything but silence.*

But he stays quiet, as if he's trying to piece together what happened between us. The silence stretches on and on, and I start to grow uneasy. If he doesn't remember last night, I'm going to die of humiliation.

• • •

If you like cocky foul-mouthed hockey players, sassy heroines and HOT forbidden sex—this is the book for you! Sexy broken alpha male Justin is willing to risk it all—even his heart for a chance with his friend's sister.

Acknowledgments

Thank you so much to my lovely readers for your enthusiasm for this couple! Dominic's arc was a tricky one, and he kept me on my toes.

I would like to thank my entire team for your support; I could not do this without you. Thank you for all the late nights and last-minute emails and handling everything with such grace. I am one lucky lady. Without my family's unending support, I could not do what I do. Thank you so much!

Up next, I have a book that is one of my very favorites I've ever written titled *Playing for Keeps*. Justin is such a swoony hero, and I hope you agree.

Get Two Free Books

Sign up for my newsletter and I'll automatically send you two free books.

www.kendallryanbooks.com/newsletter